"There's not a lot of privacy around here, is there?"

Sunny observed, wishing she could just throw herself at him and kiss him.

"You noticed," Colin muttered, eyeing her with obvious intent.

"How about your house," she said breathlessly. "Is it more private there?"

"If I took you there, it would make the weekly newspaper."

"What do other people do?" Sunny said, cutting to the chase.

"They get married…"

Dear Reader,

Welcome to another wonderful year filled with love and laughter!

First we have a fabulous screwball comedy from the talented Liz Ireland. You may be familiar with her books for Harlequin American Romance and Harlequin Historicals. In *The Hijacked Bride* she's penned a very funny story about a kidnapped bride and her reluctant kidnapper. Hale Delaney certainly never had any idea what he was getting himself into! The dialogue sparkles, the hero is to-die-for and crazy relatives abound. Enjoy!

Then we have new author Barbara Daly debuting with *Home Improvement*. Barbara wowed us with her talent. Her story about the city girl in the wilds of Vermont is a hoot! The characters are charming and warm, the romance is special and the dog, Babe Ruth, is a treasure. I'm not sure how the heroine convinced Babe Ruth to wear all the crazy outfits, but the Babe sure is one well-dressed dog! Discover the fun of home renovations!

Wishing you all the best for a wonderful New Year.

Malle Vallik

Malle Vallik
Associate Senior Editor

HOME IMPROVEMENT
Barbara Daly

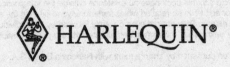

HARLEQUIN®

TORONTO • NEW YORK • LONDON
AMSTERDAM • PARIS • SYDNEY • HAMBURG
STOCKHOLM • ATHENS • TOKYO • MILAN • MADRID
PRAGUE • WARSAW • BUDAPEST • AUCKLAND

ISBN 0-373-44060-X

HOME IMPROVEMENT

Copyright © 1999 by Barbara Daly

This edition published by arrangement with Harlequin Books S.A.

® and TM are trademarks of the publisher. Trademarks indicated with
® are registered in the United States Patent and Trademark Office, the
Canadian Trade Marks Office and in other countries.

Printed in U.S.A.

A funny thing happened...

Some years ago my True Love and I built a house in Vermont. It's a great house and it must be a great relationship, because it survived the experience—barely! And that was building; remodeling is worse! It's a frustrating, maddening, apparently endless process, even when the rest of your life is more or less in order.

Sunny O'Brien's life is *not* in order. When you add in her recent divorce, a puppy, a desperate need for a place to live and a bullheaded contractor, you have a blueprint for chaos, not romance. Lurking in the margins are contractor Colin Blalock's interfering mother, who's dying to see more little Blalocks running around, and the vindictive ex-girlfriend of Sunny's ex-husband, among other confusion-causing characters. And who's trying to bring order to this project? A redheaded spitfire and dedicated city girl, and a reticent, hard-core Vermonter. Ay-uh, the job sounds hopeless!

Of course, there is Babe Ruth. Can he find a way to bring these two together? Well, there's never been a hill too high for a cairn terrier to climb. I know, because I hang out a lot with Cecily, a focused, self-centered female of the breed. She and I had a ball writing this story. We hope you have just as much fun reading it.

—Barbara Daly

P.S. To set the record straight, Cecily's only outfit is her own scruffy fur coat.

Since this is a first book, I want to thank all the people who helped me along on my journey, and you are many:

Sheridan and John and Helen for your love and unfailing support; those of you who taught me to write, Lois Anthony, Gwen Howell, Philip Lopate, Lois Walker, Barbara Kay Turner, Leigh Michaels, Lisa Reardon and the hundreds of writers and workshop leaders who had no idea how much you were teaching me; Nancy, Beppie, Wanda, Mary and Doris, my wonderful Iowa City writers' group, my world-class critique group in New York and our cheerleading local RWA chapter for reading, revising and spurring me on; to Stevie, Stephanie and Pamela, Lois, Carol and Laura for their friendship and encouragement; a special thanks to Mark Drendel of Canine Style in New York for patiently modeling dog couture one rainy afternoon.

And in alphabetical order, Mary Theresa Hussey, Karen Solem and Malle Vallik for being the best and most patient agent/editors ever.

This book, of course, is for George, an alpha male with a soft spot for kids and pets and women in distress, the hero of my own romance and the inspiration for every hero I will ever dream up.

1

Mr. Colin Blalock
Wilderness Construction
East Latham, VT 05555
May 4

Dear Mr. Blalock:

I knew better than to hire a construction firm sight unseen, and my disastrous attempt to spend the weekend in the cottage checking on your progress has proved my hypothesis correct.

You've had my *stupendous* deposit for a month. By now I thought the toilets would flush. Instead I found boxes of tile stacked on one of the aforementioned indoor facilities and the other unseated and standing in the room where I innocently supposed I could sleep. I have never slept in a plumbing supply shop, but I was willing to think about it over a cup of tea. The kitchen, however, had been stripped of its old appliances, with the new ones still standing in their boxes. The only approach to boiling water was the old wood cookstove, which I don't know how to turn on.

My general impression is that you spent my *gigantic* deposit for supplies and equipment and then lost interest. Is this the case?

SUNNY RAN A SMALL, slim hand through her fiery red hair. It crackled. "Babe. Sit. Listen to this," she said. The cairn terrier puppy gave his rubber foot with its garishly painted toenails one last ferocious squeak and sat, gazing up at her attentively with his head tilted to one side while she read the last lines aloud. "Does it sound like I'm firing him?" she asked the puppy, tilting her head to the other side. "That's the last thing I want to do!" Her fingers danced on the keyboard.

In short, after this *crushing* disappointment, I came straight back to the heat and humidity of New York and will spend the rest of the weekend walking my ex-husband's dog, Babe Ruth, who isn't housebroken yet, or Dexter probably would have taken him in spite of Marielle's allergies. This has been a bad year for me, Mr. Blalock, and after this weekend, I'm afraid it's going to get worse.

Let me explain my housing situation one more time. Through my own impatience with fine print, I admit, Dexter won our apartment here in New York in the divorce settlement and I won Woodbine Cottage, which was (still is) unfit for habitation. Ever the optimist, I convinced myself that spending a few months in my *beautifully restored* cottage, while Babe wreaked his horrible havoc outside, safe within the confines of my *beautifully restored* picket fence, would actually be beneficial to my mental health. I would then sell my *beautifully restored* cottage and buy another apartment in New York. Well, it isn't restored, beautifully or otherwise, nor does it look as though it's ever going to be. I have to be out of the apartment by July 15. Unless you are an extremely fast worker, Babe Ruth and I will soon join the ranks

of the homeless. What can I expect from you in the future?
Sincerely,
Sunny O'Brien

"That says it all, don't you think?" Babe seized the squeaky foot and growled.

Suzann O'Brien
45 East 9th Street, Apartment 14N
New York, NY 10000
May 6

Dear Ms. O'Brien:

I did not continue to work on Woodbine Cottage due to the attached letter, which I received shortly after buying the materials for your project.

As you can clearly see, the letter, written on your "Suzann O'Brien, Interiors" stationery, dismisses me from further involvement in the project. I was sorry to receive it, since it meant losing a job I had scheduled for my busiest time of year, but my next client seemed very pleased to have his restoration moved ahead.

Your deposit covered the supplies, so I left them for your builder of choice. I trust you and he or she will be more compatible and I wish you the best of luck in restoring the cottage. It is an historic West Latham landmark which I hope he or she will handle with the respect my firm had planned to give it…

"Marielle has struck again!" With a cry of rage Sunny crushed the letter into a ball and threw it at the cool gray lava wastebasket. She missed. Wagging all over, Babe Ruth chased the paper ball, brought it back and dropped it at her feet, his black eyes shining like lumps of coal. Sunny slowly unwadded the ball of paper, smoothed it out and read the last paragraph.

For the record, you don't "turn on" a wood cook-stove. First you lay a fire, then get the fire going well ahead of the cooking you plan to do...

"Oh, for heaven's sake," Sunny snapped, giving the letter another toss. "I've got to give that man a call."

From Sunny O'Brien to Colin Blalock, May 8, sent via express mail:

You don't answer your phone, you don't seem to have an answering machine, your fax and E-mail numbers aren't on your stationery and you write your letters by hand! With a fountain pen! I know the slogan—"Vermont is what America was"—but do you have to take it so literally?

Not that I'm writing in order to criticize you! I find your *modus operandi* charming—so appropriate for someone engaged in residential restoration in a state which is simply riddled with historic landmarks. I'm writing to apologize. *Naturally* you stopped working when you received the letter dismissing you from the job. I must confess that after a month went by I wondered why I hadn't received a bill from you, but I *greedily* decided to count my blessings and wait until you chose to dun me for some *exorbitant* amount that would undoubtedly knock my socks off. Have you ever had a client who reminded you to send a bill? Of course not. Nor have you ever had a contract broken, not by the client, but by *the former girlfriend of the former husband of the client*. Because the bitter truth is that *Marielle* wrote that letter! I did not!

I admit what I did to her was pretty bad...

Colin was thoroughly enjoying Sunny's letter. He paused at this point and reread the last line. "'I admit what I did to her was pretty bad...'"

What? What had she done? Now that he knew who "Marielle" was, he was fascinated, couldn't wait to find out what Suzann O'Brien had done to her archrival!

...and I feel awful about it, but when I tell you what she's done in revenge I'm sure you'll agree she's gone overboard! She has gotten hold of my letterhead stationery and is using it to harass me. She had my cable disconnected. Four days without old movies! Reconnection charges!

She changed the address on my Bloomingdale account so I didn't get the bill. What I got was a call from a collection agency! She made an appointment for me with a psychiatrist and when I didn't show up, the psychiatrist billed me anyway, which is what shrinks do, in case you didn't know. One hundred fifty dollars!

I didn't mean to get wound up in the story of my life. I cite these examples in support of my claim that *I did not write that letter* and I desperately need you to return to the restoration of Woodbine Cottage! I'm so glad we cleared up this dreadful misunderstanding!

P.S. I know you don't *turn on* a woodstove. I used the term in its broader sense. I don't intend to use the stove at all. I plan to polish it up and sink pots of herbs in the wells.

WHAT A LITTLE SPITFIRE. Colin leaned his dark head against the brown leather upholstery of his sofa, rested long, muscular legs on the coffee table he'd made from an old wooden sled and sent a grim smile toward the ceiling of his library. A sound like Niagara Falls announced the arrival of Muffler, who insinuated all nineteen pounds of his gray tabby body into the crawl space at the back of Colin's neck and gradually draped himself around Colin's shoulders. The vibration from his purr was like having a massage. It wasn't exactly what Colin needed at the moment, but it was better than nothing. He began to relax. His eyes drifted shut. He'd had a hard day. He'd sleep well tonight...if it weren't for that annoying little niggle at the back of his mind. He tried to ignore it. He told it to bug off, to no avail. Finally his eyes popped open and he sat bolt upright, sending the cat sliding down the back of the sofa with an angry snarl. What had Sunny done to Dexter's allergic ex-girlfriend Marielle?

"I'm talking about them like I know them!" He ran an impatient hand across a day's growth of dark stubble, unable to believe the depths he'd sunk to. He was participating in the drama of Sunny, Dexter and Marielle the way his mother got right into her soap operas. "It's none of my business," he instructed himself. "Sorry, Muff, let's settle down again." He leaned back and closed his eyes.

Images materialized behind his eyelids. Maybe she stormed into Marielle's apartment and caught her and Dexter *in flagrante*. Maybe she took a photographer along, or trained a camcorder on them, then released the story to the tabloids. Or: She tried to get Dexter back, and Marielle caught Sunny and Dexter *in flagrante*.

Colin's dark eyebrows drew together in a frown. He didn't like the vision he'd just conjured up, not one bit. He hesitated for a second, then reached for the phone.

"BEING WELL-GROOMED gives you a more positive self-image," Sunny lectured Babe. She sat cross-legged on the kitchen floor clipping his toenails, which he hated even more than he hated having his bangs and ears trimmed. "So stop wriggling and let's get this over with, or we'll have to start sending you to a groomer.''

The phone rang. She reached for it, and Babe scurried swiftly away. "Yes," said Sunny, more abruptly than she'd intended.

"This is Colin Blalock. I hope I'm not calling too late."

She dropped the nail clippers. "Mr. Blalock! You do use the phone! I'm so glad to hear from you. Listen. About the cottage—"

"I can't stand the suspense," Colin interrupted. "What did you do to Marielle?"

"Beg pardon?"

"I said, 'What did you do to Marielle?' I can't sleep until I know."

"You can't—" Temporarily nonplussed, Sunny took a brief time-out. "It's a long story," she warned him.

"It'll be on my phone bill," said Colin. "Give it a try."

"Well," said Sunny, collecting her thoughts, "the lawyers scheduled a meeting for the final signing of the divorce papers. Seven-thirty came and everybody was there but Dexter. Are you with me so far?"

"Mmm," said Colin.

It sounded like a yes, so Sunny raced on. "Of course I knew where to find him. We'd grown so far apart in the last months of the marriage that Dexter didn't even bother hiding his affair with Marielle, and when he moved out of the apartment, he moved in with her and left Babe with me, because Marielle said she was allergic to dogs. So I called her and she answered..."

"And you asked for Dexter—" Colin prompted her.

"—and she said he wasn't there. Then I heard a man's voice saying, 'Who's on the phone, hon?' and I said, 'Come on, Marielle, I know he's there. I can hear a man's voice in the background,' and at just that moment Dexter walked up behind me and said, 'What do you mean, "a man's voice in the background?" Give me that phone!'''

"Uh-oh," said Colin.

"Uh-oh is right," Sunny said, sighing deeply. "He made her admit she was seeing another man on the sly—of course, when he was married to me he was seeing her on the sly, but it didn't surprise me in the least to find out that Dexter believed in a double standard for men and women…"

"What happened?"

"Oh. Well. He broke up with her then and there, right in front of the lawyers and me. She considers me to blame for the breakup, and of course I was. So that's the story. Mr. Blalock," she added, eager to get onto the matter of the cottage, "while I have you on the phone…"

"Call me Colin," he said, "and the answer is no."

"Colin!" Sunny screamed. "Don't hang up!"

But the dial tone didn't answer. "Get yourself back in here, young man," Sunny yelled to Babe, "and I mean right now!" Babe didn't answer, either.

COLIN'S SMILE was less grim, more amused. He wasn't sure why, but he felt much better knowing Marielle hadn't caught Sunny in bed with Dexter.

He knew more about the characters in this particular soap opera than he'd ever let on. His mother had been hanging out the window as usual when "a cute little redhead" and a "tall, thin, scornful-looking man" came to see the cottage. The man wore a ski outfit that coordinated from wool cap to boot toe. And since his mother learned about the petite woman's divorce from the scornful, fully matched man, she had been relentlessly after Colin to make Sunny's acquaintance.

The dismissal letter had seemed like a godsend. It got his mother off his case and him back on schedule at the

Larribee place. It freed him to work where he pleased and make the acquaintance of whomever he pleased.

His smile faded. Last night he'd taken out the South Latham second-grade teacher. By ten o'clock, it seemed like the longest date he'd ever had. It was not a relationship destined to end up in bed, and Colin was more than ready to end up in bed with a good-looking, consenting, enthusiastic woman.

But not a brash, brassy, demanding city woman like Sunny O'Brien, no matter how cute his mother thought she was. Not another Lisa.

Sunny O'Brien to Colin Blalock, May 12, sent by Federal Express:

Dear Colin:

You hung up on me, you coward! I tried to call back, but, naturally, your home phone is unlisted. How *do* people reach you when they need you? Apparently something is working for you. Tell me you didn't mean it when you said no! Surely you could get me a kitchen, a bedroom and one bathroom by the first of July!

I've bought wallpaper. I've bought slipcover fabric. A seamstress in Brooklyn is hand-rolling the hems of the organdy curtains I'm going to hang at the windows. Swiss cotton, cost a fortune even with my decorator's discount! I've picked paint colors. I bought sixteen lupine and delphinium plants at the Union Square Greenmarket, for heaven's sake, and they're drooping toward me from every windowsill in this wretched apartment full of gray furniture and horrible memories!

I'm a sick woman, Mr. Blalock. I need quiet and rest and clean, cool air and Babe Ruth somewhere besides tethered on a leash I'm holding the other end of.

Call me collect to tell me you were only kidding!

In case you're interested, Dexter and Marielle are together again, after all the trouble she's caused me! Can you believe it?

"THAT POOR GIRL," cried Margaret Blalock. "Who is Marielle?"

"That poor dog," Colin muttered. "Nobody you'd know," he added in reference to Marielle. If his mother got into the story of Sunny, Dexter and Marielle she'd never get dinner on the table, and the kitchen smelled like chicken potpie.

She was reading his mail again, had fished the letter right out of his pocket while she hung up his jacket. Thank God he didn't live here with his parents—she'd probably search his room daily for interesting reading material. Should he tell her one more time that a grown man deserved a little privacy? Maybe after dinner.

"You know," he said thoughtfully, "I'd like to take that dog off her hands, give it a good home."

Margaret Blalock regarded her son with disapproval. "Colin. You're thirty-three. You're an intelligent, successful, attractive man." She eyed him again—less disapprovingly. "Considerably more than attractive, let's face it. You did not inherit the Blalock blue eyes in order to focus them on a dog. What you need is a wife."

Colin sighed. It was sex he needed, not a wife. On the other hand, in this rural pocket of southern Vermont, where everybody's business was public knowledge, it was amazing how often sex and marriage went hand in hand. And the idea of *marrying* a pushy broad like Suzann O'Brien was laughable.

Colin Blalock to Sunny O'Brien, May 13:

I was deadly serious, and I don't have time to argue with you over the phone. Our firm's specialty is restoration and we are in great demand. I cannot restore Woodbine Cottage until I have satisfied my other obligations. If you don't like walking Dexter's dog, you should consider putting him in a foster home.

Please accept my sympathy for the misfortunes that have befallen you. I wish we at Wilderness Construction could comfort you in your time of trial, but we're simply not up to it.

The lupine and delphinium should be drooping *away* from you, toward the sun. You should prepare yourself for the possibility that they are already dead.

Sunny O'Brien to Colin Blalock, May 15, a telegram:

OKAY PLANTS DROOPING AWAY FROM ME STOP YOU'LL BE HEARING FROM MY LAWYER STOP

Sunny's emerald eyes flashed fire. Restlessly she paced the apartment she'd decorated in blues, grays and whites to please Dexter. Her coloring clashed with it. The large-scale furniture made her feel Lilliputian. She could only see herself from the nose up in the bathroom mirror. She couldn't even hit the wastepaper basket!

This place didn't feel like home, and Woodbine Cottage felt more like Home Depot. Nothing was more important to Sunny than a home of her own. The last place on earth she wanted it was in the country, but she couldn't afford another apartment in New York until she sold the cottage she and Dexter had bought during a skiing weekend in Vermont. They'd been bored with each other, and it looked like a good investment. The ad had read: "Lots of charm, needs TLC." And did it ever!

Sunny's pace slowed. She sank onto the gray chenille

sofa, tucking her legs beneath her. Babe Ruth chased Bla-lock's latest wadded-up letter and brought it back to her, his tail wagging and his tongue hanging out, then compressed his little body and leaped up to join her. He'd managed to bring the paper ball with him, and Sunny clenched it in her fist.

She'd give the cottage the tender loving care it deserved, and live in it until someone bought it. Summer in Vermont wasn't exactly exile. Lots of people summered there on purpose. She wouldn't even mind if summer stretched out into leaf season. Everything would be fine as long as she could get out of the apartment by the fifteenth of July. How was she going to persuade Blalock to restore the cottage now, when she needed it?

What a bullheaded male! She could guess what he looked like—huge, silent, unshaven and none too clean in his scruffy, cluttered office as he sat down at his battered desk to pen another frustrating letter to her.

Slowly she unwadded the damp, tooth-marked ball of paper. Heavy, cream-colored stationery. Simple, elegant letterhead. Tall, spiky handwriting, unmistakably masculine. Her mental image wavered. Wouldn't the man she'd imagined scribble his letters on a notepad from a lumberyard, or a hardware store?

And his voice: on the phone, it was deep, rich and oddly reassuring. Maybe talking through a filthy, matted beard improved the quality of a man's voice, took off the hard edges.

Sunny became aware that Babe's eyes followed her every move. "Time to walk-walk?" she asked him. "Thanks for mentioning it. Don't be shy." She pulled Babe's red tartan leash from the pocket of her lime green sweats and replaced it with keys, plastic bags and a squeaky hot dog. Babe bounded delightedly around the apartment

in anticipation of the walk, but came willingly to be leashed
up, his short, fluffy tail waving in the air like a flag.

"Too bad you're not cute or anything," Sunny told him,
putting her face close to his so he could give her one delicate kiss on the nose with his tongue. "It's so warm tonight I think your red bandanna is enough, don't you? Let's
go. And none of your fighter-biter routine," she warned the
dog. "This trip to the park is strictly business!"

His request for a walk had been sincere. Apart from a
futile lunge at an Irish wolfhound five times his height and
ten times his weight, he'd kept his aggressive tendencies
under control. Gratified by his increasing dependability,
Sunny left Washington Square and sauntered east on Wa-
verly Place, taking her time before returning to the emotional discomfort of the apartment. The lighted window of
a bookstore on University Place caught her eye. Strolling
up to it, she idly contemplated the titles of the books on
display, then came to attention.

"Getting to Yes," she read. *"Your Perfect Right. Reaching Consensus."* They were assertiveness manuals, books
on the art of persuasion. *Reaching Consensus* was Blalock
restoring the house in two years. Forget it! She needed a
book called *How to Win!* And there it was: *Getting Through
a Brick Wall* was subtitled *Without getting crushed in the
rubble.* If she'd ever met a brick wall, it was Colin Blalock.

Sunny dashed to the door just as a young clerk locked
it. "You can't close yet," she said. "I just need one book.
Won't take a second."

"I'm sorry. Our hours are 10:00 a.m. to 10:00 p.m."

"I *have to have* that book," Sunny said. "Don't you
know a crisis when you see one?" She pulled the hot dog
from her pocket and held it behind her. "Bar-roo-oo!"
Babe howled.

It seemed to alarm the young man. "Okay, one book, if
you know exactly which one. You'll have to pay cash," he

demanded suddenly and very assertively, looking down at Sunny's five-two from about a foot above her.

"Of course," Sunny assured him. She was in. She raced to the pyramid of books that resembled the window display and snatched up *Brick Wall.* At the counter she dug into her pants pocket, then the other pocket, and at last gave the clerk a brilliant smile. "I don't seem to have my billfold with me," she told him, "so," she went on quickly when the clerk seemed about to say something—or throw something— "...I'll leave you my watch and bring you the money in the morning."

The clerk took the watch, looking down his nose as he handed it back. "The book's twenty bucks. I can get that watch on Canal Street for ten."

"No way!" Sunny was aghast. "This Rolex was a birthday present from my ex-husband. It's not..." She looked at the watch. "He wouldn't do that. Would he?"

"Ma'am, I don't know the guy, but I do know the watch. No dice."

"Couldn't you trust me for the money until tomorrow morning?" Sunny pleaded with him. "Look at this precious puppy." She scooped up Babe Ruth and held him close to the clerk's face. Babe dragged his tongue across the clerk's mouth. The clerk winced. "This dog's happiness depends on that book."

He gazed at Babe. "What breed?"

"Cairn terrier," said Sunny.

"Okay," he said, "I'll keep him until tomorrow morning when you bring the money. He looks pretty valuable."

Shocked, Sunny drew back, clutching Babe. "I couldn't let you do that," she said slowly, all the animation draining from her face. "He wouldn't understand. He'd be scared. He's just a baby." Defeated, she turned to leave.

"That was a test," said the clerk. "You passed."

Sunny whirled. "I did?"

"Yes." He sighed. "You're probably crazy and I'll be buying a twenty-dollar book out of my salary this week, but what the heck. Take it home."

"Oh, thank you," said Sunny. "I'll be here—when did you say you opened?"

"Ten."

"I'll be here by noon at the *latest*." She left quickly. It seemed the best thing to do.

MIDNIGHT FOUND HER deeply engrossed in the book. She lay on the gray sofa under a pink mohair throw with Babe asleep on her feet, his short hind legs spread out behind him. She'd read the admonitions to thwack the brick wall firmly and neutrally, to do so soon enough to avoid an aggressive reaction like blowing it up—and finally came to a chapter titled, "The Search for Crumbling Mortar."

"Everyone has a weakness," the author wrote, "something he cares about deeply. Study these examples of approaching an opponent through his love for cats."

Sunny scanned the examples with growing excitement. When she felt she had grasped the principle of the thing, she asked herself the pertinent question: Where was Colin's crumbling mortar? She got out the file labeled Wilderness Construction, and read through his crushed, tooth-marked and smoothed-out letters.

The answer was obvious. "Historic preservation," she croaked. Babe's ears went straight up. Blalock's letters were full of his devotion to "architectural integrity," and "handling Woodbine Cottage with respect." He hated her, but he loved the cottage. How could she exploit his fatal weakness?

Her friend Bev, who'd fled New York and moved to Manchester Village, Vermont, to throw pots, had said, "If you buy this place, don't let anybody touch it except Wilderness Construction. There are too many butchers around, like…''

She could almost, but not quite, hear the name Bev had mentioned: It began with an *F*. Frank something. Fred. Fred Franklin. No. She'd have to call Bev.

"SUNNY, WHAT'S WRONG? You're sick. You can't live with your grief any longer. The dog died. What?''

"I need help, Bev,'' said Sunny.

"Obviously,'' Bev croaked, "to be calling at this hour.''

Sunny ignored her. "Remember when you said I had to hire Colin Blalock? You said there were too many butchers around, like—who?''

"You're not going to hire him!''

"Who?'' Sunny insisted. "Who am I not going to hire?''

"I'm not going to tell you. If you let *that* man lay a hand on *that* house…''

Find your opponent's weakness. "Bev. I'm in the kitchen holding your big blue bowl in my hands,'' Sunny lied. "If you don't tell me his name I'm going to drop it on the floor. It's a slate floor, remember? One, two, thr…''

When the newly assertive Sunny got off the phone, Bev was only marginally calmer about the fate of her museum-quality pots that were in Sunny's possession. Sunny, on the other hand, was ready to negotiate with Colin Blalock.

Telegram from Sunny to Colin May 18:

LAWYER IMPRACTICAL STOP I ADMIT CASE WEAK STOP ENGAGING NEW CONTRACTOR STOP HANDYMAN NORMAN FETZER AVAIL-ABLE IMMEDIATELY STOP PRICE RIGHT STOP DO YOU RECOMMEND STOP

Colin stared at the telegram. She couldn't. She wouldn't! Thank God she'd asked his opinion! He dashed off a note and sent it by express mail.

While I hesitate to criticize a professional in my field, I cannot recommend Mr. Fetzer for restoration work. He might, with supervision, be qualified to paint the picket fence after we've repaired and sanded it. I strongly urge you to look further for a contractor to meet your immediate needs.

Sunny to Colin via Western Union on May 19:

TIME RUNNING OUT STOP FETZER ONLY ALTERNATIVE STOP HAS EXCELLENT COSTCUTTING SUGGESTIONS STOP PARTICLEBOARD PANELING TO REPLACE ORIGINAL WAINSCOTING STOP PLEASE ADVISE STOP

A scrawl dated May 19 from Colin to Sunny, and sent via Federal Express:

Particleboard paneling is excremental.

Excremental, Sunny thought gleefully. *He's cracking.*

Sunny to Colin on May 20, sent by snail mail:

Come on! The paneling can't be all that bad. Norm says you can't tell the difference. And if we use acoustical tiles on the ceiling I won't have to go to the expense of repairing all that plaster. Norm says we can just sand off what's left of those cherubs and rosettes—and he can do it all by July 8!

Colin read the letter and growled. This was blackmail! He would not give in to her! Let Fetzer butcher Woodbine

Cottage. Why should he care?

In his mind's eye Colin saw Norman hammering a crowbar under the chair railing and ripping the paneling off with his bare, filthy hands. Smiling that maniacal smile of his. With an inhuman snarl, Colin snatched up the phone, dialed Western Union and dictated his message:

CANCEL FETZER STOP WILL DO WORK PERSONALLY NIGHTS WEEKENDS STOP STRUCTURAL REPAIRS KITCHEN BR BATH BY JULY EIGHT STOP

Norman Fetzer, locally known as "the butcher" for covering two-hundred-year-old houses in vinyl siding, for slapping acoustical tile over pressed tin ceilings and for stapling cheap wall-to-wall carpeting over hard maple floors, had knocked down the brick wall that was Colin Blalock without even knowing it. "Yahoo!" Sunny screeched. "We won, Babe, we won!"

The excitement was too much for Babe Ruth. Bounding into the living room, he made a small, neat puddle in the precise center of Dexter's custom-made gray-and-white rug.

2

COLIN WAS SANDING a cupboard, half enjoying the feel of the wood beneath his hands, half mad that the owner of Wilderness Construction was sanding a cupboard on Saturday afternoon. Music from his portable CD player shimmered off the old fireplace, the wood cookstove, the new appliances in the kitchen he was remodeling for his steamroller client, Suzann O'Brien, but didn't quite mask the peculiar sounds that came quite suddenly from the front of the house.

He heard the front door open and close with an original-windowpane-shattering crash. He heard a yelp, then a squeak. He heard a moan, or maybe it was a sob. He heard words, all the more alarming because they were unintelligible, more like babbling, which ended with another slam.

It was enough to get anybody's attention. He looked out the kitchen window that gave him a glimpse of the drive. A red Jeep stood there with all four doors wide open. He clearly had a breaking-and-entering problem to deal with.

He slipped through the swinging door into the dining room, then crossed the hall to the master bedroom. He heard scuffling sounds and a repeat of the moan, or maybe sob, but he no longer needed noises to lead him to the intruder. The smell that permeated the hall, ghastly, suffocating and all too familiar, grew stronger, then nearly knocked him over as he flung open the bedroom door. He narrowed his burning eyes to slits, held his nose and honked, "Hohnt hoove, hive hot hue hovered!"

He barely had time to register the delicately heart-shaped face, enormous, sizzling green eyes, straight little nose and kissable pink lips of the girl who stood in a puddle of discarded clothing before the pink lips opened to emit an original-windowpane-shattering scream. Wild-eyed, she clutched desperately at the towel she held up to her front—apparently unaware that her back was toward the long mirror of an old-fashioned dresser.

A tangled mass of red curls fell down to thin, delicate shoulder blades. Her back tapered to a tiny waist, then blossomed into a beautifully rounded little bottom. Her legs were slim and shapely, her skin the color of heavy cream and delicately freckled. This was no girl. She was one hundred percent pint-sized woman.

Uncomfortably aware of a gathering tightness below the belt, Colin whipped his gaze away from the mirror and focused it on the small, hairy dog that sat on the bed. It was wearing a hat—a plaid tam-o'-shanter to be precise— with a matching bow around its neck. Tail wagging madly, it stared fixedly at a life-sized rubber foot lying in front of it on the bed, which explained the yelp and the squeak he'd heard earlier. Redhead, dog—the woman had to be Sunny O'Brien.

Colin struggled to recall his early training in gentlemanly conduct and eventually settled for covering his face with a tack cloth he pulled from a back pocket, wishing it were big enough to cover the rest of him. "I was kidding about the weapon," he mumbled through the cloth. "You surprised me."

"I surprised you!" She tightened the towel around herself, but it still didn't meet in the back. "This is my house! What the hell are you doing in it?"

"I work here, Ms. O'Brien," Colin pointed out.

Impossibly, her eyes widened further. "Dear God, you can't be Colin Blalock!"

He lowered the tack cloth. "Who else would be here on Saturday afternoon?"

They stared at each other until the stench forced Colin to break off staring to cough. "We meet at last," Sunny said limply, then seemed to gather herself up to attack. "Don't just stand there! Do something!"

He could think of any number of things he'd like to do if the smell weren't so strong. He settled for: "Guess he ran into a skunk. Nothing to do for it but give him a bath." He took pity on her. "I'll give him a bath," he said, "while you change...."

"Don't worry about Babe." Her tone was bitter. "He smells as sweet as a new-cut meadow. I stopped on the road to walk him, and he saw the skunk and pulled the leash out of my hand to go after it, and I chased both of them, and the skunk whirled, and I said, 'Don't you dare! That dog's fresh from the groomer!' It looked me over, then it aimed its rear end at me and sprayed me from top to toe!" She glared at him. "Stop twitching. Go ahead and laugh." She burst into tears.

When she pulled the towel up to mop her eyes, she uncovered a big percentage of the rest of her. Stunned by the brief confirmation that red was her natural hair color, Colin strode into the daisy-papered bathroom and turned the shower on full, then pulled the circular curtain around the old-fashioned claw-footed bathtub. By then he'd gotten his face, and more slowly, the rest of him, under control. "Get in the shower," he ordered her. "I'll start airing out the house."

With a last sob, she sidled toward the bathroom, and once inside, slammed the door. Colin opened the original-glass windows with great care, wondering how long they'd last with this woman around, then gazed at the legendary Babe Ruth. The dog tilted his head to one side and gazed back, then rolled over to have his stomach rubbed. Colin treated him to one serious scrub. "Come on, little guy," he said, pocketing the squeaky foot. "We've got work to do."

With two fingers he picked up the puddle of coral-colored cotton she'd been standing in and tried not to dwell on the lacy, cream-colored panties that lay beneath it. He looked around for a bra, couldn't find one but did see a small white sneaker lying in a corner. Once he'd located another sneaker on the opposite side of the room, he took the clothes to the back yard. The dog followed. Curtains twitched in the houses on either side of Woodbine Cottage. With great deliberation he spread Sunny's dress and panties over the fence that faced his mother's house, hooking the sneakers over two of the pickets. Wondering if he'd ripped the clothes off his client's body would keep his mother and Aunt Rosamond busy for a while.

Last, he dug into his kit bag and pulled out a clean T-shirt which he laid out on the bed while the shower still ran at full force. The shirt would hit her well below the knees. It would be best for his libido if she was fully covered the next time he saw her.

SHE'D HAVE KNOWN his voice anywhere if he hadn't been holding his nose, but she'd missed her guess at his appearance—by the merest trifle.

Sunny poured an entire guest-sized bottle of shampoo into her hair and began to scrub. He was tall; she got that part right. His shoulders and legs under his jeans and faded green T-shirt looked to be full of muscles. A hunk without an ounce of fat on his body. He didn't have a beard, either. His skin was smooth and tanned beneath the shock of dark hair that hung down to black brows and endless lashes, which floated down over extremely blue eyes. He was so intensely male he ought to have a testosterone warning printed on his fly.

This was the man she'd ruthlessly blackmailed into meeting her schedule? He didn't look as though he could be conned into anything.

She suddenly realized that the bathroom in which she was scrubbing herself so hard she might have been exorcising a demon contained all the amenities, soap, shampoo, snowy white towels. How did they get here? And her bedroom furniture was in place, the bed put up and made up. Had Bev gotten the cottage ready for her? Then why, when she woke Sunny up this morning to hint that she ought to get herself up here on the double to see what Colin was doing to her house, did she invite Sunny to stay with her and Greg?

Sunny's eyes narrowed. Now that she was clean, she felt up to confronting her contractor and finding out exactly what he'd been up to in the last few weeks. But she couldn't do it naked, and her bag was still in the Jeep. When she stuck her head out of the bathroom, the first thing she saw was the butter-yellow T-shirt lying on the bed. It matched the bedroom walls. She dropped her towel, grabbed the shirt and held it up to herself, turned to look in the mirror, turned back to look at the doorway where Colin had been standing, looked over her shoulder at the mirror…and sank down on the dressing-table chair, her head in her hands, her humiliation complete. "The whole time I was yelling at him," she moaned, "I was mooning him."

How could she ever face him again?

Sunny pulled herself together. By pretending it hadn't happened. If he had any manners, he wouldn't mention it, either! She yanked the soft knit shirt over her head, ran her fingers through her wet curls and went out to face the enemy.

He'd opened every window in the house, and the hideous skunk smell was fading in the soft, honeysuckle-scented breeze that blew through the center hall. She found him in the kitchen with Babe Ruth. He'd turned off the music and was sanding a cupboard vigorously enough to wear a hole in it. "Thanks for the shirt," Sunny said. "Sorry I didn't introduce myself like a normal person, but the skunk thing really threw me. I feel better now that I'm clean, and I think the house is going to air out fine, don't you?" She took a step forward—and ran into a brick wall.

"To what do I owe the honor of your visit?" His eyes, fixed on her face, hardened to blue ice.

Sunny cleared her throat. "Whom. My friend Bev, the one who came by yesterday. She called this morning and said I simply had to come," she explained, shamelessly betraying a woman she'd known since their years at the Parsons School of Design. "The house looked so great she wanted me to see it for myself." She smiled brightly. What Bev had said was: "Come up here now! Before it's too late!"

"Mmm," said Colin.

"And it does look wonderful," Sunny babbled on. "My goodness, Bev is expecting me to stay with her in Manchester Village and I don't see why I should, as lovely as the bedroom looks. Did she make up the bed?"

"No."

Some of the things you read about Vermonters were true. For example, that they tended to be uncommunicative. "Then who did?"

"My mother."

"Your mother?" When no answer seemed forthcoming Sunny added, "Please do thank her for me. No. I'll thank her myself. Where does your mother live?"

"Next door," said Colin.

"Next door! To me? Or to you?"

"To you. The house to the south." Something sparkled in his eyes, briefly warming them. It might have sprung from a murderous gene handed down by a seventeenth-century Blalock, or it might have been amusement.

"How nice. I'll meet her soon."

"Mmm."

"You and Babe Ruth seem to be getting along," Sunny ventured next. The puppy had only two personality flaws that she could detect, a neurotic fear of thunder and a psychotic lack of loyalty to her. He'd go with anybody who'd rub his stomach or throw a toy for him to catch.

"I thought he'd be larger," said Colin. "A yellow lab. With sad eyes."

"Well, now you know he's small, dark and happy."

"Right. Why is he wearing a hat and a bow?"

"Because it's too warm for his tartan jacket," said Sunny.

Colin blinked. "Mmm," he said.

"I thought Vermonters said 'ay-uh,' or something like that," Sunny said suspiciously.

"They do, until they get some exposure to the outside world," said Colin.

"I see," said Sunny, who wondered what he meant by exposure to the outside world. A trip to Boston? "So you've started on the kitchen," she said unnecessarily. "Mind if I look around?" She had to find out what had gotten Bev's tail in a twist.

Colin stood up, brushed at some wood dust on his chest and effortlessly lifted the cupboard. She followed him with her eyes as he put it down on a clean tarp, admiring the set of his shoulders, the tautness of his buttocks as he moved, sliding her gaze elsewhere before he caught her ogling him. The wood-burning stove gleamed with polish, and he'd camouflaged a contemporary gas range inside one of the old-fashioned cabinets he was sanding to satiny smoothness. Nothing was wrong; the work was going ab-

solutely right. Bev had obviously summoned her here for
the sole purpose of meeting Colin Blalock.

Matchmaking friends. God love 'em. A weekend wasted,
when she had so much to do in New York. It wouldn't be
wasted, though, if she used the opportunity to broach the
topic of his finishing the restoration now that he'd gotten
started.

She didn't need an assertiveness manual to tell her she
wouldn't succeed in a knee-length T-shirt with her hair in
a mess. She needed to sneak up on his blind side, nicely
dressed. Dressed, at least. "Now that I've seen the cottage," she told Colin, "we'll run along so you can work.
My clothes are..." she added delicately.

"...airing out on the fence," he muttered. "Here's a bag
to put them in." He handed her a huge plastic garbage bag.

"Thanks. I'll bring your shirt back tomorrow."

"I work faster without interruptions," said Colin. "Try
to schedule your inspections on weekdays before three. If
you have questions, call Trilla at my office."

"Okay, I guess," Sunny said. He was telling her when
she could come to her own house? And who was Trilla?
Colin's wife? Or a secretary, or office manager? One who
didn't use an answering machine, a fax machine or a computer? Confused, Sunny said, "Goodbye, then."

"Goodbye, Sunny," said Colin.

The way he spoke her name gave her a peculiar jolt.
When she started toward the door, Babe dug his toenails
into the smooth, wide planks of the kitchen floor and pulled
at the leash, straining back toward the warm male voice.

WORK! *Get back to work, get your mind on something besides her body in your shirt!* A miniature body, but it
mounded and curved in all the right places. By the process
of elimination, he knew she wasn't wearing anything under
the shirt, and the idea was making him crazy.

Sand a cabinet! Think about sandpaper! Rasp! Scrape!

"Isn't she cute?" said a voice behind him. His nerves were so wound up he almost flung the cabinet at the voice. He spun to find his mother and his aunt regarding him eagerly. Both tall, bright-eyed women, one fair, one dark, for a moment they looked to him like a matched pair of benign witches.

"Hello, Mother," he sighed. "Aunt Rosamond."

"Only a redhead can wear coral with such authority," Rosamond Blalock said dreamily. "But Colin, whatever had happened to her?"

"Skunk," said Colin, sanding.

Both women sniffed daintily at the air. "I told you so, Rosamond," said Margaret. "Even when she screamed I knew Colin hadn't torn her clothes off at first sight. What a picture she makes with that tiny dog."

"Mmm," said Colin.

"Now *those* genes would liven up the Blalock strain," Colin's mother went on inexorably.

Colin stopped sanding. "Mother. This is my life, not a genetics experiment."

"I know," said his mother. "But it is up to you to continue the Blalock line."

Colin's jaw tightened imperceptibly. He was fond of his mother, but she was about to drive him crazy on this particular topic. "Why didn't you have more boys?"

"God gave me everything I could have hoped for," Mrs. Blalock said piously. "Three beautiful daughters and two wonderful sons."

"And then he tied your tubes," Colin pointed out.

"Colin! That's irreverent!"

"Sorry," said Colin, and returned to his sanding. "Why don't you nag Martin to have another kid?"

"He's already had his family," said his mother.

"One child," said Colin.

"And then he had a vasectomy," Mrs. Blalock said, sighing.

"I didn't know that," said Colin, looking up from his work.

"Here you are in the prime of your manhood and you're not even trying," said Aunt Rosamond, who hadn't married and therefore had no children at all.

"I took the librarian out. I took the choir director out. I took out my tile supplier and the second-grade teacher. I'm trying."

"Did you like any of them?" his mother asked.

"No."

"See?"

Colin sighed. "Suzann O'Brien is the last kind of girl I'd want to marry," he said. "She's tough, loudmouthed—straight out of a Woody Allen movie. Her dog wears hats! She wants to sell this place and go back to New York as fast as she can. She's Lisa all over again. We don't want another Lisa, do we?" He gazed pointedly at the women.

Their expressions confirmed that they did not want another Lisa. "I suppose we should get to know her before we make any firm and fast decisions," Margaret suggested to Rosamond.

"You two," said Colin, "will not be making any firm and fast decisions about my love life, period." He went back to sanding the cupboard.

"No, dear, of course not," Margaret said comfortably. "When will you see her again?"

"Never."

"Why?" they chorused.

"I ran her off."

"Colin! You had no right! This is her house!"

"I know," Colin said stubbornly, "but..." But he wouldn't get anything done with Sunny around. He'd never be able to look at her again without seeing an image of her in the mirror, her butter-pecan ice-cream skin, the sexy little tilt of her bottom, and that image did embarrassing things to him, was doing embarrassing things to him now. "Hey, you two," he ordered, hiding his flushed face behind the cupboard, "go home and stir up some hog bristles and newts in a cauldron. I've got a lot of work to do here and not much time to do it in."

He finally got rid of them, but not until they had extorted a promise out of him. Blasted interfering women!

He liked the dog. Just like a New Yorker to dress up the poor little guy in a silly hat. He hoped she was kinder to him than she'd sounded in her letters. It was clear she hadn't wanted him.

While he sanded, he imagined a pair of vivid green eyes watching him.

"ISN'T HE BEAUTIFUL?" Bev sighed.

The washing machine finished a drain cycle and Sunny lifted the lid to see if the skunk smell was out of her clothes yet. Either it wasn't, or it was permanently laminated to her nostrils. Grimly she set the dial back to Wash and poured in more detergent.

"Thank God you're here," Greg said. "She can't stop talking about Blalock."

Bev, tall, slim and dark-haired, smiled and reached out to touch Greg's cheek. He was a jewelry designer she'd met at a crafts show, and the two of them seemed very happy living together. Only time would tell. It had taken Sunny two years to figure out that while Dexter's apartment was gray, his heart was black. "I want him for Sunny," Bev reassured him.

"I feel much better now that you're here to accept delivery," Greg told Sunny.

"Wait," said Sunny. "I sense my life rushing on ahead of me. I'll find my own men, thank you very much. You conned me into coming up here to meet Colin Blalock when Claire Lazarus is breathing down my neck to find two hundred yards of chartreuse taffeta immediately.''

"Well, sure," said Bev. "Time is of the essence. He's going to finish those three rooms and clear out. You'll go back to fighting through the mail. It might be two years before you see each other. He could be married with twins by then."

"So what?" Sunny burst out. "Let him get married. How do you know he isn't already married, to this Trilla person, maybe?"

"He's not. I asked his mother. Who's Trilla?" Bev said in one breath.

"I don't know," Sunny moaned. "You asked his mother if he was married?" She paused, gathering strength. "It *will* be two years before I see him again. He more or less dismissed me from my own house until he's through working on it. So I'm going to plant the lupines and delphinium tomorrow morning and go home."

"You can't," said Bev.

"I have to," said Sunny. "I have clients depending on me."

"I'm depending on you, too," said Greg. "If you try to leave I'll slash your tires."

"I don't have enough clothes," said Sunny.

"You're familiar with the discount stores in Manchester Center? Come on, Sunny," Bev begged. "When did you ever see a better-looking man? A healthier-looking man? A saner-looking man?"

A sexier-looking man. Sunny quickly put a lid on the thought. Sex was entirely too much on her mind these days. "I'm looking for a good-looking, healthy, sane New Yorker," said Sunny.

"People change," said Bev.

"Rarely and reluctantly," said Sunny. "It's been fun, the skunk especially, but I'm going home."

"You can't just plant those lupines and delphinium," said Bev.

"I can't?"

"Mercy, no," Greg agreed. Sunny looked up at him suspiciously, but his face showed only the gravest concern. "You'd better look for a landscape designer."

"For that little yard?" Sunny scoffed. "I'm just going to fill it up with perennials and let it…"

"The old flower beds are exhausted," said Bev. "You can see that Mrs. Forrester's plants aren't flourishing. You need to dig nutrients into the soil. You have to plan your borders for height and color and blooming times…"

"Okay, okay," said Sunny. "I'll do all that as soon as I'm here to stay."

"That will be too late," said Bev.

"Now is right but a few weeks from now is too late?"

"Absolutely," said Greg. "Vermont summers are short. Every minute counts."

Sunny glared at both innocent faces. "You know I know you're lying to me."

"Us?" they chorused.

The phone rang, and Bev darted off to answer it. "It's for you, Sunny," she called. "Colin," she mouthed. With a dreamy sigh she handed Sunny the phone.

His warm, deep voice sounded tense. "When we were drawing up the specifications for the cottage, there were a few details we didn't get around to. Where you want light switches in the kitchen, things like that."

"I guess we didn't," said Sunny. "How did you know where to find me?"

"Your friend gave me her number last night."

Sunny gave Bev a hard look. Bev returned an encouraging smile. "I see. Okay, I'll fax you an electrical design for the kitchen…" Sunny began, then remembered the maddening technological limitations of Wilderness Construction. "I have some gardening to do tomorrow before I leave," she amended herself. "Maybe we could meet at the house and finalize the, um, 'light switches and things like that.'"

"How early? Seven? Eight?"

Sunny shuddered. "About eleven. I'll be there at eleven."

"Eleven, then," said Colin. He sounded glum, which Sunny found irritating. Wasn't her fault he didn't have a fax machine. She hung up the phone and turned to glare at her hosts.

"We'd better build the fire and start the swordfish, don't you think, dear?" Greg said to Bev in a thoroughly domestic tone of voice.

"Forget the swordfish," Sunny said coldly. "Pay attention, you two. You're trying to match up apples and oranges. You know how I grew up, Bev."

"I don't," said Greg.

"Then I'll tell you. My family was so laid-back they'd make Colin look like Donald Trump. My parents were flower children. They named me Sunshine!" Sunny closed her eyes, still resenting being saddled with the name, which she'd expensively changed to Suzann.

"When they worked we had money and when they didn't…I guess it was just too materialistic to save for the lean times," she said bitterly. "They called it living the good life. For me, the good life is the rat race, ambition, drive, the things you came here to escape, the things Colin stays in Vermont to avoid. *When* I start looking…" She gave them a glare fraught with meaning. "…I'll be looking for a stockbroker or an investment banker, a man in a good, dark blue suit…"

"That sounds like Dexter," Bev said.

Sunny stared at her. "Well, then, I want somebody who sounds like Dexter, but isn't. Somebody who works with his brains, not with his hands. Somebody entirely different from Colin Blalock of Wilderness Construction!"

"He is attractive, don't you think?" said Bev.

"Yes," Sunny admitted. "He is attractive."

"He has a sexy voice."

And eyes and mouth and shoulders and legs and...

"He wouldn't have to be a permanent part of your life."

That was something to think about. "I guess a summer fling with him wouldn't be the worst thing in the world. I mean, this whole thing is a fling, isn't it? A few months in a cottage in Vermont? A brief respite from real life?" She frowned. "Problem is, I like my real life. I'm going back to New York right after I talk to the man about light switches."

"What are you going to wear tomorrow?" said Bev.

"Something more than a towel," said Sunny. "Let's go see what I packed."

3

MORNING SERVICE ENDED at the Congregational Church of West Latham, across the green from Woodbine Cottage. Bells gonged a farewell hymn as parishioners streamed through the big arched doors. One group detached themselves from the crowd, and began walking in the general direction of Sunny's yard. There was a tall, handsome, graying blond woman at their center. Sunny envied the way they laughed and talked together, casually touching or flinging an arm around one of their companions for a brief hug.

They were obviously a family. As they came closer, four of the group gripped her attention. They had to be the woman's children. Except for their dark hair, they looked just like her. Three females and one male—Colin. She felt like a heathen orphan standing under the old sugar maple tree, staring over the fence at them as they scattered toward the line of cars parked in front of the Blalock house, waiting to see which one owned the classic yellow Corvette she'd been admiring.

"Goodbye, Mother," said the women, kissing the blond woman before sorting out husbands and piling children into the cars. "Bye, Colin." When the amenities and the departures were finished, Colin and the yellow Corvette were left over. This was an unexpected development.

Another surprise was Colin's appearance. "Hi," she said as he silently unlatched the side gate and came into the yard. He wore a well-tailored dark blue blazer with gray slacks and a white turtleneck. You'd never guess he was Mr. Wilderness of Wilderness Construction, particularly when you imagined him roaring away in the yellow Corvette.

"That was your family," she said. She'd meant it to be a question, and was embarrassed when it came out as a sigh.

Colin whipped his eyes upward from his contemplation of, Sunny was sure, the grass stain she'd already gotten on her white jeans. "Mmm."

"You go to church together." Wasn't that same scene in her first-grade reader?

"We have breakfast together and go to church. A tradition that goes back five generations." He sounded rebellious. "In my mother's family. Speaking of whom…"

Sunny turned to see the tall blond woman advancing through the front gate. "Mother," he said. "This is my client…"

"Oh, I know. Hello, Sunny. I'm Margaret Blalock. I won't keep you," Mrs. Blalock said warmly. "Just wanted to say hello before I ran off to the estate sale."

"Thank you for making up my room," said Sunny. "It made me feel right at home."

"We'll have you over soon," Mrs. Blalock promised, "to meet the whole family."

"I'll look forward to it," Sunny murmured. Way forward, she hoped.

Colin seemed annoyed as his mother said fluttery goodbyes and climbed into a van, presumably serious about the estate sale. His eyes locked on Babe, who was in his country outfit this morning, a sleeveless denim jacket and a bandanna. He looked very smart, and Sunny wondered why Colin was glaring at him, but her mind was on the happy family scene she'd just witnessed.

"Your mother's a blonde and the rest of you are dark-haired," she observed.

"She's a Latham," he said as though that explained everything. He was still gazing at Babe.

"It figures," Sunny said. Lathams, Blalocks, Carters, Forresters, Twombleys—all she'd have to remember were first names and who was married to whom. "I didn't see your father. Is he…"

"At his physical peak. He left at dawn for an auction in Calais."

"It looks like a nice family to belong to."

Colin swiveled away from his contemplation of Babe to give her a glance so quizzical that Sunny was afraid her voice had given away her wistful envy. But he responded with a shrug, stooping to pick up Babe's squeaky foot. He gave it a powerful toss down the side of the house, watching Babe scamper after it delightedly. "What? No hat?" he said.

"I don't want the neighborhood dogs to think he's a sissy."

"All New York dogs wear hats?"

"Um, no. He sort of stands out there, too."

"Aren't you afraid you'll warp him for life?"

"Oh, for heaven's sake," Sunny snapped. "He's a dog. When he's six months old I plan to warp him so thoroughly the hats won't matter one way or the other."

Colin blanched. "If you don't mind, let's not talk about it," he said. "Let's talk plugs and switches. I have a lot to do this afternoon."

She watched his delicate manipulation of the huge old key, saw him run his hand across the sanded surface of the front door and frown. He pulled a small notebook from his shirt pocket and wrote himself a note.

Sunny craned her head. Naturally, he wrote with a fountain pen. The note said, "res. fr.dr." Resand the front door.

A perfectionist. When he paused to give the inner door the same treatment, she wandered into the living room to examine the plaster ceiling. "This was a formal house for its time, don't you think?" she called out, groping for conversational topics. "The other houses I looked at didn't have sculpted ceilings or wainscoting and molding this ornate."

"Mmm," said Colin. "The Forresters always have been uppity. It was built later than my folks' place, some Forrester daughter's wedding present. A starter home, so to speak."

"You're telling me my house isn't old by West Latham standards?" Sunny found this news upsetting.

Colin gave her one of his slow blinks, long lashes feathering out over his cheekbones. "I wouldn't call 1826 cheap new construction," he said.

She followed him to the kitchen. It wasn't a small room, but his maleness crowded her, kept her hovering at the doorway to keep from crashing into his chest. She suddenly felt nervous. "You aren't going to work in that blazer, are you?"

"No," said Colin, "I'm going to draw little rectangles on the walls in my blazer. Then I'll change clothes and get to work. Where do you want the switches?"

His brisk attention to duty was annoying. After seeing his family, Sunny felt an urge to learn more about him, and he didn't look very chatty poised with a pencil in his hand. On the other hand, there was a certain advantage to his dignity. Nothing in his demeanor toward her indicated that only yesterday she'd treated him to a full view of her derriere in living color—before she'd even said hello.

Maybe it wasn't dignity; maybe he hadn't liked the looks of her derriere.

"A light switch at this door and the mudroom door and the back door," she said hastily, "and the dining room door and the pantry door and the door to my bedroom. My goodness, there are a lot of doors.''

"Mmm," Colin murmured. He reached around her to mark the wall near the doorway. The faint scent of balsam wafted past her nose. Sandalwood soap. His hands were long and tapered, the fingernails broad, neatly clipped and very clean.

"This is standard height. Do you want it lower?" He bent toward her as he asked the question, and their faces were just inches apart.

Her breath came a little faster. How many generations of Latham-Blalock blood did it take to produce eyes that blue, teeth that even and white? "I'm not *that* short," Sunny said. "Of course I want the switches at standard height."

A ghost of a smile crossed his face. "You got it," he said. She watched him cross the kitchen to make more neat rectangles. His shoulders shifted slightly from the pent-up energy in his stride. She stepped a little farther into the kitchen and was staring at him when he turned toward her again. "Outlets?" he said.

"Excuse me?"

"Where do you want wall outlets?"

"Oh. On the walls, of course, at the usual intervals."

"Do you use a lot of small appliances?"

"I have a lot of small appliances," Sunny said. "I can't say I use them."

He gazed at her for a moment. "You will here," he said, and began to draw rectangles above countertop level.

"Maybe I will," Sunny acknowledged. "It might be fun to learn to cook a few things besides pasta and brownies. That can be one of my summer projects."

"Don't bother," said Colin, his back to her, "unless you want to eat."

"I guess there aren't a lot of restaurants," Sunny conceded.

"Twenty miles is a long way to drive for breakfast," said Colin.

"Oh." She'd better go back to the bookstore and buy a basic cookbook. "I need someplace to plug in a coffeepot."

He gave her another of his inscrutable gazes. "Any of these will do."

"And a microwave and a toaster."

"Right," said Colin.

She walked toward him, feeling more at ease now that he'd become so talkative. "And another phone jack and a cable hookup."

"No cable," said Colin.

"No cable?" Sunny thought briefly about life without news and old movies. "A plug for a VCR," she said.

"Carters' rents videos," Colin supplied, reading her mind.

"I know," said Sunny. Twenty-three of them, fourteen of which were classic Disneys. They'd be great for Babe, but what was she going to do for entertainment? "And Babe needs a doggy door," she added, because if you looked at it from a certain perspective, a doggy door was an outlet. "Should he have two? One in the kitchen door and one in the…"

As they both reached toward the lower half of the kitchen door their hands brushed. Sunny felt a frisson of electricity run up her arm. His skin was so warm, even in the coolness of the room. "…back door?" she finished breathlessly.

"Doggy—" He cleared his throat. "Pet doors aren't in the contract."

"I know," said Sunny, "but I need one so Babe can go out by himself."

"I could do it summer after next," said Colin.

She had no intention of being here summer after next. It was time to bring up the topic that would turn this wild-goose chase into a worthwhile business trip. "You've done a great job," she began. "I can see why you're in such demand."

"Mmm," said Colin.

"You can't leave it half-finished," said Sunny. "You must want to see it in its final glory as much as I do." She gave him a confident smile.

"I want to finish the Larribees' work."

"But surely you could fit this work in at odd moments…"

"I've been working sixteen-hour days to get you a kitchen, a bedroom and a bathroom," interrupted Colin. "I can only do that a few weeks at a stretch."

"I know you must be tired," Sunny said soothingly, "and I'm not asking you to go on working such long hours. But you have a crew. You could supervise…"

His hard blue gaze froze the rest of the sentence in her throat. "Good people are hard to come by. I've committed them to the Larribee house."

"Please think about it. If you have to import higher-paid people, I'll…"

"Mine are higher-paid people. The answer is no."

"Think about how nice it would be to have me off your list, all happily settled in a house that's ready to sell…"

"No."

"I could offer a modest bonus…"

"I don't need more money."

How could anybody not need more money? "What if you finish the kitchen and put in the doggy door, and then we talk about it some more?"

"No."

"Maybe Norman Fetzer could do the doggy door," Sunny suggested.

A muscle in Colin's jaw twitched. His eyes darkened to indigo. She smiled encouragingly. He frowned back.

"Not in this door," he muttered. "The back door."

"Okay," Sunny agreed. "I'll tell Norm to chop a hole in the back door."

Sunny followed his gaze to the door in question, which opened from the back yard into the mudroom. It was one of the original maple kitchen doors. Colin had cleaned it and rubbed it down until its warm, glowing patina was restored. She imagined Colin imagining Norman Fetzer hacking at that door with a saw, maybe even a pickax, an expression of manic glee on his face.

Colin's sigh was like a fierce arctic wind. "Find the door. I'll install it."

"Thank you," Sunny said warmly. "I'd much rather have you do it."

His "mmm" sounded different when his teeth were clenched. "And that's it," he said. "No more additions to the contract, or wheedling or blackmailing…"

"Blackmailing," Sunny gasped. "How dare you accuse me of blackmail?"

"I am a restorer of houses," Colin said coldly. "I am not a fool. Now if you'll excuse me, I have work to do. For an extremely demanding client!"

IT WAS BLACKMAIL and he'd fallen for it again! Colin snarled softly to himself as he got out of his dress clothes and into jeans. No, it wasn't as though he'd fallen for it, he'd simply agreed to pay! If she let Fetzer lay a hand on this house, he'd…

Zipping his jeans, Colin grew thoughtful. They were loose—when there weren't any half-naked women around. He'd lost weight working this job, and sleep, and unbelievably, his customary sense of being in control of his life. This morning he'd spotted a gray hair springing out of the black. It had to stop.

His eyes went to the rotary phone he'd brought over to

use until Sunny supplied the house with her own phones. He picked up the receiver. He dialed.

"Norman," he said. "Colin Blalock. Hey, Norm, how well do you know this Sunny O'Brien you've been negotiating with?" Colin smiled contentedly. His conscience didn't hurt a bit. He'd caution Norman that Sunny was a tough taskmaster, that she demanded itemized bills, that she was always *in a hurry* to get the work done. That ought to banish the threat of Norman, who worked when he felt like it, charged what he needed to live on until he felt like working again, and did not take kindly to orders given by women. Colin's smile faded.

"You don't? You've never talked to her?" A frown creased his forehead. "Sorry to have bothered you, then. At Sunday dinner, too. Pork roast. I'm sure it is good. Better get back to it before it gets cold. See you, Norm."

She'd never even spoken to the guy! That clever, conniving little...

Colin glanced out the window. He'd let her know in no uncertain terms how he felt about being conned. Doggy door be damned. Dog could ruin the hardwood floors before he'd...

No, he couldn't risk the dog ruining the floors. He'd add in the pet door and that was it. He'd been giving the Larribees half measure long enough as it was. Colin peered down the fence line past a hole somebody had dug that was big enough to plant a crabapple tree in and caught a flash of white that had to be Sunny. But she wasn't alone. *Oh, hell. Aunt Rosamond's latched on to her.*

TEMPORARILY STONEWALLED, Sunny had retreated to the garden. Babe greeted her delightedly, his denim coat filthy and his bandanna hanging in shreds. There were burrs in his tail. "Look at you," she told him. "Is this the way you intend to look all summer?" She dusted his coat and took off the bandanna, then went to the car to get the pretty hand tools with the bright green handles she used to loosen the soil around her houseplants. "Let's get the planting done and get the heck out of here. Your groomer's going to up the price when she sees you."

Moving purposefully to the back of the perennial border that lined the fence, she plunged the trowel into the soil where she'd decided to put the first delphinium. It sank to a depth of one inch and stopped. Sunny braced herself and shoved harder. The trowel bent. Straightening it out as best she could, she moved a little to the right. This time the trowel emitted a hideous scraping sound. Her teeth on edge, she stood up. She needed a shovel. There were rocks in her yard.

"Gardening is a challenge here."

Sunny jumped. A tall woman with Colin's coloring stood on the other side of the picket fence. "I'm Rosamond Blalock," the woman said. "Colin's aunt. His father's sister. The family spinster," she added comfortably.

She was hemmed in by Blalocks! "Hello," said Sunny. "I'm Colin's client, his nemesis, a major pain in his big thick… I'm sorry," she added hurriedly, "I shouldn't have said that about your nephew. It's this soil I'm mad at."

She was relieved when Rosamond Blalock laughed, and unnerved when she said, "We all know who you are. Yes, indeed, our Vermont soil takes some working. I'm here to help you in any way I can."

"Thank you," said Sunny, touched by this neighborly offer. "First of all, how do you dig a hole?"

"Ask your puppy," said Miss Blalock. "He's dug quite an ambitious one beside the *Rosa rugosa*."

"Oh, my G— Oh, my," said Sunny, glancing frantically in the direction Miss Blalock was looking, toward the back of the house. "Where is he now?"

"He's fine," said Miss Blalock. "He has Margaret's cat

Clarabelle treed. See? Over there in your beautiful old maple?''

''Babe! No! You mustn't chase Mrs. Blalock's kitty.'' Sunny dashed to the scene of the crime. Babe danced around the tree on his hind legs while a cat, either extremely fat or extremely furry or both, glared down at him from the first fork in the tree.

''Clarabelle's in no danger,'' Miss Blalock said comfortably, ''and she'll keep the puppy out of trouble while you and I talk soil.'' As Sunny gazed dubiously back at Babe, her neighbor went on authoritatively, ''I expect you've struck rock. You'll have to dig out a lot of rocks. Then you must add a dressing of manure.''

''Manure?'' said Sunny, her attention diverted from Babe and Clarabelle.

''Yes. Horse manure's best, but cow dung's all right.''

''Are the stores open on Sunday?'' Sunny asked, feeling faint. ''I've got to get this work done and go back to the city.''

''Oh, my dear,'' said Miss Blalock, ''you're not talking about an hour's work. You need to spend a week or so digging the manure in, and you must water thoroughly. Don't want to burn the roots of these old plants.''

What would the manure do to her? ''I don't have a week,'' Sunny said, ''not this week anyway. I could get the manure and some tools, and then I could work enough soil to plant these...'' She gestured toward her row of plants.

''You can borrow all the tools you want from me,'' Rosamond said kindly.

''How nice of you,'' said Sunny. ''Maybe just temporarily. Where do you buy manure?'' She could imagine the trip back in the Jeep after she'd hauled manure to the cottage. ''It does come in bags or something, doesn't it?''

"Yes, but we all order it from Ed Carter," said Rosamond.

"He delivers?" Sunny's mood brightened. Delivery in
return for a generous tip was a way of life she understood.

"Of course. Colin knows his number. And dear, don't
buy any more plants. I can give you all the lupines and
delphinium you want. Do you know veronica?"

"No," said Sunny, hoping Veronica was a gardener-for-
hire. "Do you know Trilla?" she added as an afterthought.

Rosamond Blalock seemed startled by her question.
"Trilla's my great-niece," she said, looking confused,
"Colin's brother's daughter. She's helping out in Colin's
office this summer. But how did we get on the subject of
Trilla? I was talking about veronica. The perennial. I have
several wonderful varieties you're welcome to. They make
such a nice statement in the border."

"I do like a plant that makes a statement," Sunny said.
She was surprisingly glad to know Trilla was family. "All
right..." She almost called her Rosamond, and somehow
knew it wouldn't be the right thing to do on such short
acquaintance. "—Miss Blalock, I'll order manure, and
when I get back in a couple of weeks I'll accept your kind
offer of plants and tools and all the advice you can give
me."

Miss Blalock's smile was entirely too satisfied for
Sunny's comfort as she went toward the house in search of
the telephone, Babe following closely behind.

In the kitchen was an old black rotary phone Colin must
have supplied. Feeling like an interloper, she peeked in. He
had changed into jeans and another faded T-shirt. This one
was pink. It turned his hair raven blue-black and his eyes,
which confronted her accusingly, almost purple. At least
something had turned them purple.

"Your aunt told me to order manure from Ed Carter,"
she explained. "She said you knew the number."

His voice was cool, and he didn't look happy, but he recited the number and she dialed. A man answered. "Mr. Carter?"

"Ay-uh."

"This is Suzann O'Brien. I own the..."

"Ay-uh."

Sunny blinked at the receiver. Was there anyone in West Latham who didn't know who she was? "I'd like to order some manure."

"Horse or cow?"

"Horse," said Sunny, remembering Miss Blalock's suggestion.

"Full, half, quarter."

Sunny turned to Colin, her hand over the mouthpiece. "What does he mean, full, half, quarter? Your aunt told me to get pure horse manure. Should I say full?"

Colin was silent for a moment. "Yes," he said finally.

"Full," said Sunny.

"Green or composted," said Ed Carter.

Sighing, Sunny covered the mouthpiece again. "Green or composted?" she asked Colin. He'd gained interest in the conversation, must have, because he'd stopped working altogether. "Green would be fresher, wouldn't it?"

"Ay-uh," said Colin.

Sunny gave him a curious glance. He'd reverted. "Green," said Sunny. "When can you bring it?"

"Tomorrow," said Ed Carter, "round two."

"Colin..." She turned back to him. "Will you be here tomorrow afternoon to give Mr. Carter a check?"

"Nope."

He didn't explain, and Sunny felt stuck. "All right," she said. "I guess I can be here." If she dug manure in until dark she could still get to New York by midnight, get up bright and early, start calling around for that damned chartreuse silk taffeta...

"Where d'ya want it?"

"In my yard," said Sunny, trying not to sound impatient. Where did he think she wanted it? In the bathtub? She hung up the telephone. "All set. I guess I have to stay until tomorrow." She gave him a sidelong glance, still hoping for reprieve.

He smiled, but the smile was a slow curve that made Sunny oddly uneasy. He went back to work, attaching the original tin drainboard to a countertop, but the smile remained.

He knew something she didn't. It was really quite unnerving.

4

It was the squeaky hot dog on her face that woke Sunny up. "Ahh. What is that blinding light? Oh. I suppose it's the sun. Walk-walk?" she groaned.

Ripe cairn-terrier breath on her cheek confirmed her suspicion that a walk was just what Babe had in mind. She went out into Bev's yard with him and took a tentative breath of the fresh, clean air of a Vermont summer. It was invigorating. With renewed energy, Sunny strolled across the grass in her flimsy cotton robe, comparing Bev's emerging flower borders with her own. The manure would make all the difference. In a couple of years Bev would be begging her for gardening tips.

But she wouldn't be gardening at Woodbine Cottage in a couple of years.

Fully awake and alert, Sunny brewed coffee as a surprise for Bev and Greg, showered and put on the last garment left in her bag, a petal-pink linen sundress. One eye on her watch, she said good-morning to her hosts and retreated to their guest room with her cellular phone. She called her home number to retrieve her answering machine messages, listening nervously to a barrage of calls from Claire Lazarus. She was in trouble. She dialed Claire's number.

"Sunny, darling, where have you been?"

"In Vermont. Just for the weekend. Everything's under..."

"Sunny, angel," said Claire, "I'm calling because we

need to speed up the redecoration. We're having a little political benefit dinner on the thirteenth.''

"Of what?" said Sunny.

"July," said Claire. "Can you get the curtains by then? And the rugs. The entertaining areas have to be presentable.''

Her apartment had been quite presentable before Claire entered her fifties phase. "I'll try," Sunny said. She shuddered at the thought of the interior she had worked out so carefully for Claire—chartreuse silk curtains, fuchsia shag rugs and all the accessories to complement the truckload of fifties furniture Claire described as a steal. She was going to decorate her own new apartment in chintz and lace. In fact, she'd furnish the cottage that way, and when it sold, she'd move the decor directly into the apartment. It would work out so nicely, if only Colin would—

"Try very hard," she heard Claire saying. "I have a lot of friends who are bored with their decorators' same old ideas. They keep asking me how you're doing. They keep saying, 'But does she have the connections to do the job right and do it fast?' They're waiting, Sunny. They're waiting for my recommendation.''

Claire had certainly found her weak spot: professional ambition. "I'm sure you'll be delighted to recommend me," Sunny said smoothly. "July 13?" It was quite impossible. "The apartment will be perfect for your party, Claire. Stop worrying.''

She called the next silk mill on her list, then another silk mill. It was too late for custom dyeing. She had a nightmarish vision of trying to dye two hundred yards of taffeta herself. Giving up on silk for the moment, she called the rug supplier.

"Delivery's scheduled for August first," the man told her cheerfully. "I can put a rush on them. It'll cost you an extra, oh, about…"

The excess charges would come out of Sunny's profit, but that was part of the game. Claire's friends were the Upper East Side group she most wanted to work for; they decorated extravagantly and often. Sunny gritted her teeth and went back to searching for silk.

"SILK?" SAID Rosamond Blalock. "Around here? Wait, let me think. Carthage, that's it. Discount fabric stores. But I'm sure they won't have anything you want."

"No, probably not," said Sunny. She and Miss Blalock were in the garden shed matching shovel to gardener in anticipation of the manure delivery. Sunny put a sneaker that had been snowy white the day before yesterday atop the rusty shovel head and pushed. "This feels comfortable," she said.

"It should," said Miss Blalock. "It was my grandmother's favorite. She was about your size. No, as I was saying, you won't find anything suitable for New York in those stores. They still have fabrics from the fifties."

"What?" said Sunny, thrumming with sudden excitement.

"That's right. All those neon colors, you know..."

"I certainly do," said Sunny. "How far away is this town?"

"An hour, I suppose."

Sunny glanced at her watch. It was after one. "Miss Blalock," she said winningly, "would you do the most *tremendous* favor for me?"

Holding a check for Ed Carter, Rosamond stared after Sunny and Babe as they took off at breakneck speed for Carthage. Stopping at one textile outlet after another, Sunny at last found a clerk who remembered some silk taffeta. "Nothing you'd want," she said, but Sunny insisted, and the two of them spent an hour rolling bolts aside in a warehouse whose history as a barn was still very much in evidence, at least to the nostrils.

"Here it is," the woman called. "My goodness, look how much of it. But it's…"

"Chartreuse," Sunny breathed when she ripped open the brown paper roll. "I'll take it."

"All of it?"

"All of it. How much is it?"

"I think Mr. Bacon'd feel mighty lucky to get five dollars a yard for it. There're a couple of bolts of that fuchsia color, too. Want those?"

Sunny would have felt lucky to get it for a hundred. Bothered by her conscience, she insisted on paying twenty-five. She drove back to West Latham with fourteen brown-paper-wrapped rolls standing up in the back of the Jeep. She'd drive the fabric to New York and hand-deliver it tomorrow to her special secret seamstress whose name and number she shared with no one. She'd trim the chartreuse curtains with fuchsia bands. Claire would be…

Sunny drove past her house, stared, and drove all the way around the green before she had the nerve to edge up the driveway that separated her yard from Colin's mother's. Still staring, she parked behind Colin's truck.

In her front yard was a mountain of the vilest-looking substance she'd ever had the pleasure of owning. It stood as high as the big front windows. It covered the grassy space within the flower borders and spilled over onto her brick walk. If spread out evenly over the flower beds—it would be unthinkable!

She got slowly out of the car, still staring. A neatly coiffed graying head peered around the mountain. "I told him you wouldn't have asked for a full load," said Miss Blalock. She sounded nervous. "But he insisted you had. And I told him you surely asked for composted manure, not…not…*this,* but again he insisted, so I paid him. I hope I did right.''

Sunny hadn't closed her mouth for several minutes. Now she did, but only to gather volume. "Colin!" she bleated. "This is his doing!"

"Colin? No, dear, it was Ed Carter. Colin hadn't arrived yet. He's here now, of course, but…"

Sunny clenched her teeth. "What did Colin say when he saw it?" she asked.

"Nothing," said Miss Blalock. "He just gave me a smile and went into the house. It was a rather odd smile, now that I think of it. Why do you ask?"

Hot bolts of fury rushed up from Sunny's feet to her scalp. She knew her face must be scarlet. She rushed back to the car to let Babe out, and with a warlike cry, surged up the brick walkway, intent on tackling Colin.

The battle cry segued into a scream when her sneaker met a mound of manure. She slipped, fell down and slid another foot into the mess. Angry, frustrated tears filled her eyes as she sat on the walk, her pink dress filthy, her sneakers stained beyond repair.

Colin chose that moment to emerge from the house. "Just can't seem to stay clean, can you," he remarked.

"You…" Sunny remembered just in time that Miss Blalock still looked on. "You did this to me," she yelled. "You told me to order a full load. You told me to…"

"Correction," Colin said. "You asked me what I thought you should do. And this…" he waved at the pile "…is what I thought you should do." He came down the steps and advanced on her slowly, taking in her disheveled appearance with that same maddening smile growing on his face, then reached out a hand to help her up.

"Don't touch me," Sunny said in a low, threatening voice, "or I'll call the cops."

"Cop," said Colin.

"Singular?" Sunny said. "This town has one police-man? Wait. Let me guess. I bet you're related to him!"

"Nat Latham's only a distant cousin of Colin's," Margaret Blalock spoke up unexpectedly from her side of the yard.

"A cousin," Sunny moaned. She fixed a withering gaze on Colin, whose smile was now full-blown. "I've heard of tricks like these," she said, gathering steam. "Vermonters think it's funny to pull these stunts on flatlanders who don't know any better. Well, you just listen to me, Colin Blalock. This is the last trick... Babe, get down from there!" she screeched.

From Babe's point of view, the mountain of manure was a cairn supplied entirely for the pleasure of a certain cairn terrier. Happily he wagged a matted tail at her from the top of the heap before racing down and back up again. Sunny caught a glimpse of his paws. The manure clung to them. He looked as though he were wearing boots under his little overalls. She groaned and closed her eyes.

"Let's talk about Norman Fetzer," said Colin from a great height. She opened her eyes. He folded muscled arms across his chest and glared down at her.

The jig was up. He had discovered that a flatlander had played a typical trick on a Vermonter. "I can't possibly have this discussion from this position," she said with great dignity. "Your face is out of perspective."

"Maybe we don't need to have the conversation at all." His voice was dangerously calm.

"You mean we're even."

"Mmm."

Sunny sighed. She glanced at her car full of chartreuse silk, then at Babe, who was merrily rolling over and over down the mountain. She couldn't go back to New York leaving her yard covered in green manure. Slowly Sunny stood up, once again waving away Colin's outstretched hand.

"I'll be back tomorrow to deal with…this," Sunny said to the Blalock women. "Try to ignore it until then." How, she wondered, could they possibly ignore such a major topographical feature?

"You can't get in the car like that," Rosamond said. "We'll find you something to wear. Colin, maybe you have another clean shirt in that bag of yours. Margaret's and my clothes are much too large. I'll get some old towels for the puppy to sit on."

Sunny drove home to Bev's cries of distress in the faded green shirt Colin had been wearing when she first met him. It felt good against her skin. Was it her imagination, or did it smell ever so faintly of balsam?

"DID I BRING UP my son to mistreat women?" Margaret said sternly.

Colin glared unrepentantly at his aunt and his mother. "The devil made me do it," he said, "the redheaded one who just drove away."

"We have to help her move this pile," said Margaret. "It will burn the grass."

"I could use a little manure," said Rosamond. "Couldn't you, Margaret?"

"I could indeed," said Margaret. "What a good idea, Rosamond."

The women parted for their respective homes leaving Colin on the walkway, his arms still folded across his chest. Why did the little firebrand have to look so sexy in his shirts? Strangely unsatisfied in spite of his overwhelming victory, Colin stomped inside to work until exhaustion sent him home.

SUNNY SHOWERED, bathed Babe and scoured both tub and shower. Next she put everything she and Babe had been wearing into Bev's washing machine. In a robe of Bev's she drifted through the kitchen, where Bev and Greg gazed at her silently as they cooked, to their mudroom, where Greg had helped her stack the rolls of taffeta.

"Dinner's ready," Bev said gently.

"Go on without me," Sunny murmured. "I have to work."

"You have to eat," said Bev. "I won't let you get any thinner."

"If I must spend my days shoveling...horse indiscretions," she said in a too-calm voice, "then I have to decorate houses by night. Decorating houses is my source of income. It is the key to my success and happiness."

"If I had a pill, Greg, I'd give it to her," said Bev.

"I have some stress tabs," said Greg. "Vitamin B. That couldn't hurt her."

"Would you get me one, sweetheart?" Bev said anxiously. "Make it two."

They eventually talked Sunny into sitting down for dinner, where she picked at the risotto with asparagus and mushrooms as though it were hay. "This is excellent," she said politely. "Is it hard to make?"

"Yes," said Bev.

"Oh, well," Sunny sighed. "Just curious."

Her hosts exchanged a glance. "Sunny," Bev said carefully, "everything is going to be fine. Greg has volunteered to wrap your fabrics for shipping and take them to UPS tomorrow morning. We'll send them by overnight delivery. Your curtain-maker will have them almost as soon as if you drove them to New York."

"That is very kind of you, Greg," Sunny said thoughtfully. "Since I am being held prisoner here, I need good friends like you. May I help with the dishes?"

"No," said Bev, clutching one of her hand-thrown dinner plates to her bosom.

"May I be excused?"

"Yes. Sunny, I feel that you have something important on your mind."

"I do," said Sunny. "I'm regretting my past and reorganizing my future."

She returned to her room, Babe trailing along behind her. He was exhausted from cairn-climbing and was soon asleep in the precise center of the narrow spool bed in the guest room. While she unrolled and rerolled each bolt of taffeta, making sure it hadn't suffered any damage during its long storage, her mind whirled feverishly.

She didn't need a psychiatrist or even a stress tab; she simply didn't deal well with uncertainty, never had. She couldn't build a career in the city by working at long distance. No one would buy the cottage now; the word would spread that the only decent contractor in the area wouldn't complete the restoration for two years. She could rent an apartment in New York until she had enough cash for a down payment, but the rented place would have to be made livable, and rent was money down the drain.

Finally too tired to think in circles any more, she pushed Babe over gently and got into bed. She closed her eyes. The image that appeared behind her eyelids was not chartreuse curtains, but Colin.

He had looked so big and solid confronting her on the sidewalk with his arms folded across his chest. His jeans snugged around his masculinity, and even as mad as she was, she'd wanted to run her fingertips through the crisp black hair that sprang from the open neck of his denim shirt. Most of all, she had wanted to take the hand he held out to her, to let him help her up, to laugh with him about the dirty trick he'd played on her, to apologize for the dirty trick she'd played on him.

Instead, she'd fought back, the way she always did. Wishing she could stop fighting, just for a minute, she fell into a stuporous sleep.

THE NEXT MORNING Sunny made a stop at Carters' Store to buy a pair of jeans. While she was there, she asked Emily Carter if she had an infant seat in stock, enjoying the woman's startled expression. The rumor would spread by noon. "No, but we do have a baby carrier," said Mrs. Carter. "The kind you wear on your back."

Sunny examined it. It was made of soft canvas. If she slung the straps over the headrest, and if Babe would agree to ride with his hind legs sticking out of the little openings at the bottom, he'd be much safer in the car. She completed her shopping and went on to the cottage.

"Vigilantes!" she moaned when she pulled up in front of the house. The yard swarmed with women, probably there to complain, to ask Sunny to move out of the neighborhood, to string her up from the sugar maple tree for defiling their immaculate environment. No, worse! They pushed wheelbarrows! She was literally going to be tarred and feathered and carried out of town in a cart by the women of West Latham! And there sat her erstwhile friend Rosamond at a folding table, undoubtedly collecting names on a petition!

Babe went directly for the manure pile. Sunny slowly approached the table. "Three dollars is enough for that load, Celeste," she heard Rosamond say to one of the women. "Plus, of course, an hour's work here."

"What is going on?" Sunny gasped.

"Good morning, Sunny," cried Margaret. With difficulty Sunny located her in the side yard digging manure into the soil. "Come and meet the neighbors. We're sharing the load of manure, and everyone's helping you work yours in."

The manure pile was half its original size. "Wait," said Sunny. "You mustn't...I can't let you..." She paused and took a deep breath. "Give back their money," she directed Rosamond, then addressed the bright, interested faces of her new neighbors. "Take all the manure you want," she said expansively. "My treat."

For a moment she listened to the cries of halfhearted protest. "I will be back to help," she said, "as soon as I've changed into my, um, my yard clothes."

"We'll watch the puppy," Margaret said comfortably. "He's having such a good time. May we take off his baseball shirt? It's getting awfully mucky."

"Don't bother," said Sunny. "I brought a fresh shirt he can wear home."

She'd found a pair of boys' jeans that she gathered in at the waist with a chrome yellow braid belt, also from the boys' section. Her red T-shirt said, West Latham Volunteer Fire Department. She admired her new image in the oval bedroom mirror while she pulled her luxurious hair up into a careless ponytail and secured it with a pink elastic, still frustrated that Carters' hadn't had a yellow one.

Ready for gardening, Sunny started for the door, only to be assailed by worry about her future. She meandered through the house, looking at the tremendous amount of work that had been done and the even greater amount still to be done. The ceilings needed repairs, and the moldings. The walls needed plaster work as well, and the floors should be sanded down to the bare, beautiful maple Colin had matched so perfectly in the kitchen. The mantelpiece around the parlor fireplace was rotted beyond saving; it should be replaced, and the old brick of the hearth scoured. The window frames, the pediments over the doors...

A memory of her father came back to her. When he chose to work, he was, in fact, a skilled carpenter and finisher. He was taking care of her one day while her mother played the guitar at a folk festival, and she'd helped him repair an old door pediment not unlike the one over the cottage parlor door. It had pulled apart; he had put it back together like a jigsaw puzzle, involving Sunny in the delicate, tedious work as though it were a game.

Her glance shot from ceiling to woodwork to floor. If her father could do it, why couldn't she? *What's so hard about restoring a house?* There were books to tell you how to plaster and sand, how to scrape clapboard and repaint it, how to…

The glorious end of her incarceration in Vermont shone ahead of her like the famed Olympic torch. She knew exactly how she'd get this house in shape and sold so she could get on with her real life in the city. She'd do the work herself!

5

"PLASTERING IS not that easy," Bev warned Sunny. "Let me repair the cupids."

"No," Sunny said firmly. "You are not going to do the cupids and Greg is not going to restore the woodwork. Your jobs are to throw pots and design jewelry. Mine is to do cupids and woodwork. What can be so hard about it?" she asked Bev as she packed gleaming new tools into a bag like the one Colin carried. "My father does stuff like that. Colin does stuff like that, for heaven's sake."

"Colin has experience—and a degree in architecture from Princeton," said Bev.

"Colin went to Princeton?" It was unbelievable. "Where did you hear that?"

"His mother told me. Proudly. Undergraduate in history, then architecture."

"His mother! You asked Colin's mother about his educational experience?"

"Of course not. She volunteered it."

"When?"

Bev swallowed. "When she invited you to spend the Fourth with them."

"The Fourth of July? And you told her…" Sunny held her breath.

"I told her you'd love to. She asked us too, but I told her we had plans."

"Bev! How could you? The whole day?"

"The whole day, the whole Blalock family. They have their annual reunion on the Fourth."

Sunny gazed wildly at Bev. "They must number in the thousands! How can I spend a whole day with a thousand total strangers?"

Bev alarmed Sunny by lowering her gaze to the floor. "Mrs. Blalock worried about that too. So she wants you to come to breakfast before church on Sunday."

"Breakfast? Church? I was planning to spend the weekend in New York! I need to pack! I need more how-to books! I—"

"—will feel much more comfortable if you've met the immediate family. I told her you'd love to."

"No!" Sunny wailed. Her eyes narrowed. "It's a plot," she said. "You and Margaret Blalock are determined to get me together with Colin, when we are the two most different people…"

"I'm sure this has nothing to do with Colin," Bev said, but her eyes shifted untruthfully. "She's seen so little of you lately she was afraid you'd gone back to New York. You're a new neighbor, she likes you and she wants to be hospitable."

"She wants you for her son," said Greg.

"Greg!" said Bev. "You're not helping."

"YOU DID WHAT?" Colin froze, one booted foot on Sunny's driveway, one still in the truck. His eyes narrowed. "It's a plot," he said. "You women are determined to throw Sunny and me together. It's not going to happen! All we have in common is the cottage, and all it means to her is a down payment on a place in New York!"

"This has nothing to do with you," Margaret Blalock said, examining her thumbnail. "She's a new neighbor, I like her and I want to be hospitable." She paused. "She can bring the puppy to breakfast, but I'm afraid he wouldn't add to the worshipful mood at church. Should I talk to her about it?"

"Yes," said Colin, "before she buys him a little clerical collar."

"Colin," his mother said reproachfully. "You know Congregational ministers don't wear clerical collars."

"A tiny New Testament then!" Colin raged. "You've gone too far, Mother. I'm not coming!"

"You have to, dear," his mother said comfortably. "You know your father will be at an auction. It's your job to be the head of the family, to carry on the tradition of five generations…"

Muttering to himself, Colin went to work on Sunny's kitchen. What could she be up to? He hadn't seen her in days, and it made him madder than hell to realize he was missing her.

"PUT YOUR FOOT through that hole," Sunny ordered Babe, "and leave it there." Babe responded by scrabbling so violently he almost spilled out over the top of the baby carrier. "Sit on your tail," she insisted. "No wonder you're not comfortable. Is that better?" More scrabbling. "Babe," said Sunny, taking his face in her hands, "do you want to *go* in the car with me, or *stay* here with Aunt Bev and Uncle Greg."

The scrabbling ceased. With a heave of his body, Babe sent his tail and back feet out through one of the openings, clutching the top hem with his front paws. "You're so smart," said Sunny. "Let me see you in your new hat. Oh, you're adorable." She started the engine. "Are we ready for this new adventure or what?"

An hour later, gazing at a crumbling wall in the cottage parlor, Sunny felt confident that they were up to the task that lay ahead. First of all, they had a correct working wardrobe. Babe was so cute in the hard hat she'd found in a toy store in Brattleboro, and the little white canvas overalls were just too much. She'd found them at the Gap, of all places, in Burlington, where she also unearthed a treasure trove of striped T-shirts to round out his summer wardrobe. The baby sizes fit him beautifully. There weren't many dressy things, of course, but he didn't need them in Vermont.

Her white painter's pants vied with Babe's overalls for chic practicality. They didn't come in boys' sizes, but Sunny had belted in the smallest pair Carters' had and rolled up the legs. Her sneakers, already a total loss fashion-wise, served as her working shoes. She'd topped off the outfit with one of Carters' plain white boys' undershirts and protected her hair with a bandanna.

But work clothes were only the beginning. A gigantic sack of dry plaster, delivered by a sympathetic merchant after he'd sized her up, sat in the middle of the parlor floor. She owned a set of professional tools that had been ungodly expensive. She had a book, *Plaster Repair to the Historic Home,* to consult if she felt the slightest doubt about what she was doing. She'd covered the floor with several plastic tarpaulins, and she'd borrowed Colin's ladder. He'd never know; she'd have it back in place and be out of here before he came to work on the cottage this afternoon. She'd start with something easy—repairing a wall. Following the directions carefully, she mixed a bucket of plaster.

The plaster was interesting stuff, soft and squishy. Babe took one look at it and knew the meaning of "adventure." "Babe, look at you," she exclaimed. "How did you, when did you…come here, young man, and let me clean that stuff off your face. Stop squealing," she admonished him when he greeted her cleanup attempts with a series of throaty yelps. "I hope you've learned your lesson. Now stay out of the plaster. I have serious work to do!"

A few hours later she sat back and gazed at her handiwork. She had done quite a nice job of the roughing coat on the first wall, very smooth, very neat. Nothing to it. She could continue working on walls, now that she'd mastered straight plastering, or she could experiment with the cherub frieze.

Why not? Sunny positioned the ladder under a cherub in an inconspicuous corner, trotted up and down the ladder a few times with tools and a freshly mixed bucket of plaster, shooed Babe off the ladder and was ready to begin.

Some time later she leaned back and decompressed her tense spinal column, conceding that it wasn't as easy to sculpt a cupid as it was to plaster a wall. In addition to the artistic challenge, there was the gravitational challenge. Her bandanna was literally plastered to her hair. Babe had most unfortunately gotten in the way a few times and bore the evidence on his hard hat and overalls. And if she wasn't mistaken, his tail was wagging very slowly, as though it were weighted down.

However, the first cherub was finally shaping up. She'd followed the original lines as much as possible, using one that was in fairly good shape as her model, and the body looked rather fetching. The face needed more work, though. Her tongue between her teeth, Sunny worked doggedly at the damp plaster.

"What the hell are you doing?"

She dropped the shaping tool. "Colin! I didn't expect you here so early." She gave him a sweet smile, hoping it would distract him from noticing that she was using his ladder.

Colin ignored the smile, stalked over to the ladder, raked a glance across its plaster-smudged rungs and looked up at the cherub. His eyes widened. "It looks like—" His voice rose to a thunderous roar. "It looks like Danny DeVito!"

Sunny tilted her head to examine the cherub's face. "It does rather, doesn't it? My goodness."

In stormy silence, Colin took in the whole scene, the book, the tools, the bucket of plaster, Babe in his hard hat and overalls. When he brandished the shaping tool at her, his blue eyes flashing, Sunny imagined fifteenth-century Blalocks storming across an English meadow brandishing axes. "This house is not a joke!" he said in a low, dangerous voice. "I will not let you destroy it!"

He thought she didn't take the house seriously, when nothing could be further from the truth! Her feelings hurt, she went on the attack. "What do you mean you won't let me," she yelled back. "This is my house! I'll do whatever I want to it!"

"No, it isn't your house!" Colin's voice carried better than hers when he wasn't half trying. "This house belongs to the history of this town, this state, this nation! You have a responsibility to maintain it as part of that history!"

Babe's black eyes flickered uncertainly between Sunny and Colin. Sunny felt sorry for him and wanted to say something soothing. On the other hand, she would applaud a little show of loyalty on his part, like taking Colin's foot off at the ankle.

"I have a responsibility to get my life in order!" she cried. She was so mad, she was close to tears. "I have a career to worry about. I have to fix up this house so I can sell it and go back to New York where that career is! I can't hang around for two years waiting for you to…to make cherubs that don't look like Danny DeVito!" She grabbed the shaping tool from his hand and stubbornly lifted it to the cherub's face.

"Don't touch that ceiling!" Colin shouted.

"You can't stop me," Sunny snapped.

"The hell I can't," said Colin.

Sunny shrieked when strong hands gripped her waist and lifted her away from the ladder. She clung to the top rung, kicking and flailing, but his hands were like a vise beneath her breasts as he closed in on her, trapping her legs against the ladder. Then one arm went around her, and his other hand was wrenching her hands loose from the ladder, to grip them both in one of his, to turn her toward him and then, at last, to slide her resistant body down the length of his to the floor.

Except that her body was no longer resistant. It felt like a melted pool of butter skimming down his muscled frame. The bandanna slipped from her head and her hair fell free around her shoulders. Her breasts, bare beneath her shirt, tingled from his touch, their nipples hard and sensitive. She wriggled against him and was rewarded by the tightening of his arms as he pulled her more tightly to him. She felt his arousal pressed against her stomach, and when she looked up at him in surprise and mute appeal, he kissed her.

His mouth came down to brush hers lightly, as though he were trying to hold himself back. His touch was electric. She closed her eyes to wait out the shock. The kiss deepened, sweetness and quickening passion, antagonism and fondness all in one soft, enveloping caress. She sank into the hardness of his chest, his flat, muscled stomach, and felt herself lifted off her feet as she responded to him. For a moment suspended in time his mouth roamed hers, his tongue flicking into the corners and then, at last, into the wet warmth beyond. She moaned, going wild inside and wanting, wanting—

Almost anything, except to feel her sneakers firmly planted on the floor again. "I'm sorry, Sunny," Colin said. His voice was rough, and he backed away from her, his eyes dark with alarm. "Really, I'm very sorry. I don't know what came over me. This isn't like me. I assure you I won't touch you again. I am truly very, very—"

"The devil made you do it," said Sunny. Dazed and rattled herself, it was the first thing that popped into her mind. When she saw the startled expression on Colin's face, she realized it was no time to tease him. "You don't have to apologize," she said, her voice shaky. "It just happened." And she wanted more to happen, damn it. It was frustration that made her say, "If you'll excuse me, Danny DeVito awaits." She spun and put a foot on the bottom rung of the ladder, hoping her legs were steady enough to climb it.

"No!" said Colin. "No." She paused. "Get down off my ladder and do something you know how to do." His voice sounded as unsteady as she felt. His eyes raked the room again. "Look for light fixtures. A chandelier! And a mantelpiece! Yes! Find a mantelpiece to replace this one. You should be able to do that. You're a buyer, remember? Not a builder. I'll…" He paused, ran a hand across his forehead and gave her a look that was strangely helpless for a man as big as he was. "I'll send my plasterer out Monday morning if you'll promise not to touch that ceiling again."

Sunny took her foot off the ladder and turned to stare at him, her green eyes brimming with sudden tears. "You will?" she said. "You'll let him fix the ceilings, and repair the walls, and…"

"One thing at a time," Colin grated.

"Oh, Colin," said Sunny, a smile hovering around her mouth waiting to burst forth, "thank you!" Excited, she flung out her arms toward him.

"Call me when you find a mantelpiece," he said in a strangled voice, backing away. "No! Don't call me! Leave a note. I'll get to work now. And for God's sake, see if that book of yours says how to get the plaster out of Babe's tail. He clanks!"

With one last glance that said volumes, he strode toward the kitchen, clearing his throat, and closed the door behind himself.

Well, Sunny thought, *well.* Feeling spacy, she remembered joking with Bev about a summer fling with Colin not being the worst thing in the world. Could it be that she was about to find out?

WHAT HAD POSSESSED HIM? Colin crouched silently near the baseboard, his head sunk in his hands, unwilling even to grind maple-tinted wood filler into the dent until he was sure she was gone. The minute he'd closed his hands around that tiny waist he'd been in trouble. The minute he caught sight of her he'd been in trouble! Did she have any idea how that undershirt outlined her bare breasts? They were perfect little…peach halves, he thought insanely, each one topped with an unripe raspberry. Ah, he was losing his mind. No, merely misplacing it.

Did she have any idea how long he'd been without a woman? He'd practically attacked her! He stood up, straightened, and fought down his instinct to kick another dent in the baseboard. He'd been so embarrassed about his obvious lust for her that he'd given in, dammit, again! There was just something so appealing about the faint freckling on that creamy skin—

"BABE, COME HERE at once! You're torturing that poor cat!" Within seconds of arriving at the Blalock house for breakfast, Babe treed Clarabelle on top of the refrigerator.

"Clarabelle can take care of herself," Margaret Blalock said. "Sunny O'Brien, this is Colin's sister Kate. Blake, the tall one in the yellow sweater, is her husband, and this is Belinda, *our* youngest, with Scooter, *her* youngest, and here we have Fiona and Fred, and Belinda's husband, Carl…oh, and here's Trilla," Rosamond Blalock said, pulling the tall blond teenager close for a hug.

Sunny felt dizzy. The parlor, dining room and kitchen of Margaret and Martin Blalock's house swarmed with their progeny, and Sunny swirled through them in the long silk skirt and cropped peach chenille sweater she had bought in desperation the day before just to have something different to wear. She'd never sort these people out. How could she organize all those blue eyes that gazed at her so rapaciously?

"She wants you for her son," Greg had said. At the moment, she thought he might be right. She felt like a piece of fresh meat, sensing a hidden agenda in the family's compliments and interested questions. Babe stole the scene in his little white shirt and paisley bow tie, having the time of his life with children his own age to play with. Everyone was being so nice to both of them.

Except, of course, Colin. He obviously didn't want her here. He steered as clear of her as he could in these close quarters. She felt a little embarrassed each time she caught sight of him, the memory of their moment of passion all too sharp in her mind. She felt tender, sensitive to the touch. Good thing she'd worn a bra.

"I'm sorry Martin's not here," Mrs. Blalock sighed when she had gathered her brood around the huge oval dining table. "He says Sunday's the best day for auctions and estate sales. Do you think it's just an excuse to skip church?"

"You've been married to him for thirty-eight years," Colin pointed out. "You must have noticed that Dad always gets out of going to church one way or the other. Was it just last winter he took up ice-fishing?"

"My dad has already picked up Grampa's tricks," said Trilla. "I sort of like all this." She made a sweeping gesture that seemed to take in the family, the town and beyond. "Dad's the black sheep of the family, you know," she explained to Sunny.

"Trilla doesn't mean Martin Junior has misbehaved,"

said Mrs. Blalock. "He just didn't take to the family traditions the way the rest of my children did. He…"

"He practices law in Boston, where he has become outstandingly successful and extremely wealthy," Rosamond said sadly.

A general hum and sigh went around the table. "He's not happy," said Kate.

"No, indeed," said Mrs. Blalock. "All he does is work."

Sunny could barely hide her amazement. They were serious! Martin Blalock Junior had broken loose from this backwater town and gone to Boston to make something of himself, and they thought of him as the family black sheep, while Colin dribbled his life away as a country contractor to his family's full approval. The Lathams and Blalocks might be as deeply rooted as her parents were nomadic, but apart from that, they reminded her entirely too much of her own family. She felt like scooping Babe up and whisking him back to the real world of drive and ambition before he caught this insidious country virus and started cuddling up to cats!

But she couldn't, because it was time for church. The sisters waved away her offer of help as they cleared the table of scrambled eggs and ham, biscuits and sticky buns, pale yellow creamery butter and jams that gleamed translucently like stained glass. Babe was left with a bowl of water and a row of plates to lick, and Sunny O'Brien was off to church for the first time in fifteen years.

She didn't know how Mrs. Blalock maneuvered her into the pew beside Colin, but there she was, sharing a hymn book with him and shivering a little each time their hands accidentally touched. He had a nice bass voice, to which she added her lilting soprano. Emily Carter of Carters' Store, almost unrecognizable in a wildly flowered hat, played the organ. The sermon was not the hellfire-and-brimstone sort she'd supposed it would be. Instead, it was about the importance of helping those in need so the government wouldn't have to. Altogether, the experience was quite painless except for the sense of Colin beside her, his arms folded across his chest, touching but not touching, and the eerie feeling that the entire congregation was paying more attention to them than to the minister.

This time she crossed the green with the large, happy family, briefly pretending she belonged to them. She told everyone goodbye, avoiding Colin's eyes, and thanked Mrs. Blalock.

"We'll see you bright and early on the Fourth," Margaret reminded her. "Colin will pick you up at seven. We don't want to be late for the parade in Randolph."

"What?" said Colin.

"Dress casually," his mother hurried on. "Wear something cool, but bring a sweater. You never know..."

"The Fourth of July?" said Colin.

"...what the weather will be like," said Mrs. Blalock. "Colin, do get Scooter down from my clematis trellis. It's not all that stable..." The smile she gave Sunny as she shooed her in one direction and Colin in the other was nothing short of smug.

HIS MOTHER HAD STRUCK again! Colin gunned the Corvette into action and set out to meet his father at the auction in Windsor. Well, this time she might hang herself from her own organdy apron strings. A full day of Blalocks, of watermelon and rhubarb pie, of small-town parades and small-town people, and Sunny would go screaming back to New York.

Then he could go on with his life. He hoped his contribution to the church this morning would cover the lustful thoughts he'd been enjoying. Soon, though, the disturbing effect of Sunny's inviting reflection in the mirror would

wear off and he could sleep through the night without toss-
ing and turning, waking up drenched in the sweat of hot
frustration. He'd take another look at the choir director,
maybe the tile supplier. As for the second-grade teacher, a
literal woman with no sense of humor, no sparkle, a neat,
sensible hairdo and no freckles, she was definitely out.

6

"YOU MUST BE the plasterer."

A slim man of about Colin's age, he gave Sunny a brief smile. "Yep," he said. He reached into the back of his truck for a bag of tools.

"You're not from around here, are you?"

"Nope." He started toward her front door. Sunny scurried along beside him.

"Your name isn't Latham or Blalock or Carter or..."

"Ted Rollins," he said, finally pausing to hold out his hand. His eyes were a rich, dark brown, not the color Sunny had come to think of as Blalock blue.

"What a relief," Sunny said, "to meet someone who's not related to Colin."

"We went to college together." Ted set the bag down on the front stoop and returned to his truck for an armload of drop cloths. Sunny dogged his steps.

"In the school of architecture?"

"History."

Sunny leaped in front of him. "Then why are you plastering?"

"Can you think of anything better to do with a degree in history?" He walked around her as if she were a shrub and carried his supplies up the front steps.

Sunny tagged along. "You could be writing books," she suggested.

He came to a sudden stop. "Aw. You know. Colin told you."

"Know what?"

He sighed. "My wife and I write historical romances. I do the history, she does the romance. Plastering is our day job."

"Colin knows such interesting people," Sunny said limply.

"Wait'll you meet the plumber," Ted said. "He's out of prison on work release. I'd better get to work. Colin said start with a cherub that looks like Danny DeVito."

"WANT TO GO ANTIQUING?" she asked Babe a couple of hours later when she'd gotten the interior design portion of her life in order. She was quite aware that it was the word "go" that made him start dancing in circles around her, but she was pleased, nonetheless, to find him so open to enriching experiences. She said goodbye to Ted, who had turned Danny DeVito into a Michelangelo masterpiece, put Babe into his car seat and set off into the countryside.

The mountains were lushly green. Drifts of daisies and wild mustard bloomed in the meadows, peppered with the orangy dots of Indian paintbrush; wild Queen Anne's lace lined the narrow roads. The sky was as blue as any pair of Blalock eyes, and the air was cool and fresh. Retreating from the sunlight into the dim, dusty shops along Route 7, she found tables and glassware, lamps and high spool beds, primitive cupboards and benches. She bought chandeliers for the parlor and dining room that had once held candles. She bought a bed and dresser for the guest room and a beautiful old secretary for the parlor. Mantelpieces, however, were in short supply.

When she'd begun to wonder if she'd ever find the one thing she really needed, a dealer on Route 100 said, "Your best bet's the Red Barn in Latham Center."

"Ten minutes from my own front door," she said as she parked beneath a sign proclaiming The Red Barn and below that, Architectural Salvage. "This is going to be it, Babe, I can just feel it," she told the puppy. His tail wagged through the carrier opening. Sunny lifted him out and clipped on his leash. "Let's see what we can find."

"Looking for anything special?" said the dealer. He was gray-haired with blue eyes that twinkled as his gaze traveled from his potential customer to her dog, then back to her. Babe often made people's eyes twinkle.

"A mantelpiece," said Sunny, "appropriate to the early eighteen hundreds."

"Don't get many of those," he said, sliding off his tall stool.

"You don't have anything?" Her hopes had been too high. She felt let down.

"Didn't say that. Said I didn't get many. Got a great one right now."

He led her to a back room filled with corner cupboards that had once been built-in, doors, iron gates, stained glass windows, clawfooted tubs, pedestal sinks—and an absolutely wonderful mantelpiece. Plain and simple, the mantelshelf beautifully beveled, it could have been made for Woodbine Cottage. Silently, Sunny examined it. It was made of maple, with a sheen that came from being touched by generations of hands. "Where did it come from?" she breathed.

"They tore down a house in Windsor," the dealer said sadly. "Shouldn't have, but they did. I bought the doors and such. Just brought it in Sunday."

"How much is it?" Sunny asked. The price was right. "I'm pretty sure I can use it," she said. "I have to check with my contractor."

The dealer gazed at her for a moment, apparently making an internal decision. "Check with him as soon as you can," he said finally. "It'll go fast."

"Could I leave a deposit?" Sunny asked, feeling anxious.

"Don't need a deposit. I'll hold it a day." His mouth twitched. Sunny hoped the twitch wasn't a serious nervous condition. It seemed to be quite uncontrollable.

"Thanks," she said. She measured the mantelpiece, then gave the dealer her card. He barely glanced at it, his eyes twinkling all the more brightly.

Colin was working at the Larribee house. Since she hadn't the faintest idea where it was, she set out for East Latham to leave a note with Trilla, as ordered. She was there before she realized it might have been West Latham, it was so similar. She drove around the village green, past a steepled white church, and cast an admiring glance at a trim white cottage set back from the brick street by a vibrant blue-green lawn ringed in flowering perennials. There was a sign on the picket fence, whose white paint was peeling in a most charming way. Expecting a historical marker, Sunny got out of the car to read it. It said Wilderness Construction. Use side entrance.

Sunny looked at the house. Its front door was painted sky blue. An addition on the side that appeared to be as old as the main part of the house sported a second blue door which bore a small brass plaque. Sunny moved purposefully toward it and knocked on it.

"Come in." It was Trilla's voice. Sunny opened the door to see the teenager sitting behind a computer. "Ms. O'Brien," said Trilla. "Hey, it's great to see you."

"I thought Colin didn't have a computer," Sunny said.

"He does now," said Trilla. "I updated him." She grinned at Sunny. Her blond hair was pulled back into a ponytail that swung from side to side as she moved. "It was a struggle, let me tell you. But when I showed him how easy it would be to keep his inventory and do his payroll, he was hooked."

"More time for fishing," Sunny said.

"Uncle Colin doesn't fish," said Trilla. "Or hunt. He reads."

"How interesting," said Sunny, revising her image of Colin one more time.

Interest grew in Trilla's eyes. "Would you like to see his library?" she asked.

"I don't think I should tour his house until he shows it to me himself," Sunny said. "I mean…" She blushed.

"I know what you mean," said Trilla.

Sunny wanted to get out before the conversation took any more wrong turns. "May I leave a message for him? I think I've found our mantelpiece."

"Want to tell him in person?" said Trilla. "I'll give you directions to the Larribee house."

Sunny might have been tempted if it hadn't been for the manipulative expression on Trilla's otherwise sweet face. Another matchmaker; they started early in this family. "We communicate much better in writing," she said firmly.

When she didn't hear from Colin the next day, Sunny decided to take a chance and buy the mantelpiece anyway. If it didn't fit, she could probably resell it in New York for three times the price. After buttoning Babe into a red-checked shirt that would coordinate nicely with his tartan leash, she left for Latham Center. As she wheeled into the driveway of the Red Barn, her eyes widened.

The dealer and a tall, dark-haired man were loading her mantelpiece into a battered pickup truck. It was Colin's truck, and the man was Colin! Sunny's quick temper exploded. "Unhand that mantelpiece!" she yelled, leaping from the car.

They almost dropped it. Clutching at it, they lowered it to the ground and turned as though they were attached by hinges to face Sunny's rage. "What are you doing?" she asked Colin. "That's my mantelpiece. I found it."

"I read the note," said Colin, "and I knew..."

"You," Sunny lashed out, "were going to buy it and resell it to me at one of your usual inflated prices! Well, think again!" She turned furiously to the dealer. "How could you?" she reproached him. "You promised you'd hold it for me. You people all stick together, don't you. You should be ashamed!"

"Well," said the dealer, "I..."

"Now I'm here," Sunny announced, "and I demand to buy this mantelpiece."

They stared at her in silence. "Okay," Colin said finally. "It's yours."

"Good," Sunny said briskly. "I'll write a check." She returned to the Jeep, grabbed her checkbook and let Babe out. He scampered happily toward Colin. When Sunny caught up, waving his leash, he was rolling on the grass at Colin's feet, begging to have his stomach rubbed. That precious dog had the loyalty of a carp!

"You do deliver, don't you?" she asked the dealer, her pen poised.

"Ay-uh." He paused. "That'd be extra."

"How much extra?"

The dealer's eyes began to twinkle. "Hundred dollars."

"One hundred dollars!" Sunny gasped. "That's outrageous!"

"That's the price," said the dealer.

With a show of assertiveness, she could get herself out of this. She turned to Colin. "You're on your way to the cottage," she pointed out. "You could deliver it."

"Ay-uh," said Colin. He paused. "That'd be extra."

Sunny gritted her teeth. *"How much extra?"* She'd never noticed before how Colin's eyes twinkled, even now, when he wasn't smiling.

"One twenty-five," he said.

"Ah!" Sunny breathed. She stared at Colin, and then at

the dealer. The twinkle in their eyes was entirely too similar.

"I can't undercut my father's price," Colin said mildly.

She pivoted neatly on her heel and marched away without looking back.

"Got a terrible temper," Martin Blalock remarked, watching the Jeep wheel erratically out of the drive.

"Mmm," said Colin.

"Your ma's got a bee in her bonnet about that girl."

"No kidding," Colin said dourly.

"I can see why."

"Not you, too!"

"You're outvoted," his father said. "You better talk to her about that temper, though. Woman like that could make a man miserable."

"You're telling me," Colin muttered.

"When she's not making him mighty happy," said Martin Senior. "Come on, son, give me a hand with this mantelpiece."

HUMILIATED, Sunny decided she couldn't face Colin in the morning without a new, confidence-building dress. In Manchester Center she found a light blue denim sundress trimmed in red plaid with an amazing red plaid sweater edged in light blue denim. She bought new white sneakers, a white straw hat with a red band and a vivid red straw handbag, a huge one she could climb into if she embarrassed herself as badly as she had today.

Still half asleep, she was wearing it all when she answered the door the next morning. Babe was in red, white and blue, too, and disgustingly happy to see Colin. Bev and Greg hovered in the kitchen doorway wearing the hopeful smiles of parents sending their daughter off on her first date. Sunny could have killed them.

Colin put her into the passenger seat of the yellow Corvette, took Babe from her arms and looked uncertainly toward the back seat of the convertible. "I'd better put the top on," he said.

"Don't bother. I have his carrier with me," Sunny ventured, diving into the massive handbag. "If I hook it over the headrest, he can ride in front with us."

He held the carrier at arm's length, gazing at it. "Okay," he said. Across the barrier of Babe's furry face, he gave her a smile.

It was a smile of forgiveness. Sunny melted a little inside. "I, um, overreacted yesterday," she confessed. "I'm sorry. I've been tense about so many things, I guess I just lost it—at the most inappropriate time."

"You sure amused my father," said Colin. "He and I found the mantelpiece at the auction on Sunday, but I told him I'd better not take it until you'd seen it. You found it yourself before I could tell you about it, and the rest—" he sighed deeply "—the rest is your introduction to Martin Blalock Senior's bizarre sense of humor."

"I'm happy to have brought some pleasure into his dreary life," she said.

"And to mine?" Colin asked.

"I know you didn't want me to come along today," she said defiantly, thinking he might be referring to her infiltration into his family life, "so I'd like you to know I had nothing to do with it. Your mother invited and Bev accepted."

"I've changed my mind," Colin said quietly. "I hope you have, too." His hand closed lightly over hers.

Sunny's pulse quickened. His gentle touch was more sensuous somehow than their sudden, frantic kiss had been. The conflict between hostility and desire was gone. There was only affection in this caress, and Sunny felt herself relaxing inside it. His hand was warm; the calloused tips of his fingers were smooth rather than rough, and suggested the strength of the man in their light grasp. With her sense of relaxation came the warm throb of something more than affection. Her own fingers arched, sliding up through his to spread them apart. She shivered, felt the car lurch. "I'm not complaining," she said, but the words lacked her usual breeziness.

"I have something to show you when we get to West Latham," said Colin. His voice was husky. He cleared his throat. "Won't take a minute."

Thirty minutes later Sunny gazed at the mantelpiece, completely installed. It glowed against the smooth white plaster walls, and overhead, cherubs with sweet baby faces smiled down upon it. Colin must have worked half the night to put the mantel in place and repair the granite fireplace facing. "It's beautiful," Sunny said, feeling unusually humble. "I don't deserve it after the way I acted."

"No delivery charge," said Colin.

"Now that," said Sunny, "maybe I do deserve." She sent him a sidelong glance.

"No charge for the mantelpiece either," he said. "Dad wants you to take it as a gift. He says it belongs in Woodbine Cottage. It's his contribution to history."

He handed her an envelope. She knew her check crinkled inside. She started to protest, then thought better of it. Instead she turned her face up to Colin's, her lips parted, and moved a step closer. His breath came faster, his arms opened.

"I don't know what to say," she whispered.

His gaze shot toward the front door, his face underwent a transformation; his arms dropped to his sides, he sighed. "Say, 'Hello, Mrs. Blalock,'" he suggested.

"Sunny! Good morning!" crowed Margaret Blalock as she bustled into the cottage parlor. "Isn't the mantel beautiful? Colin worked half the night on it. Come on, you two.

We have to start out for the parade!''

The Fourth of July had begun with a bang.

"HOW MANY MORE of you are there?" Sunny asked an hour later.

"We've picked up about all the Blalocks who're going to the parade," Colin said as a blue van pulled into place in front of him. "This is Woodstock, so that van's my cousin Taggett's. That just leaves Aunt Joan in Barnard.''

"Compared to the Lathams," Sunny said, looking ahead toward the growing caravan of cars and vans, "the Blalocks are practically Gypsies.''

"I guess so," said Colin. "Too many of them for you?"

"I feel pretty safe in here. When we have to get out of the car, I don't know. Why should we bother going to a parade anyway? We are one. And you," she said, giving the Corvette's gleaming dashboard a pat, "win the classic car prize.''

Colin looked surprised. "I never thought of it as a classic," he said. "It's just my car. It's always been my car.''

"You've only had one car?" Sunny was astounded. Dexter ran through cars like so many paper plates.

"It was my father's midlife crisis car," said Colin. "Then it was Martin Junior's first car, and when he went away to college, it was mine.''

"I cannot in my wildest dreams imagine your father having a midlife crisis," said Sunny. "What were his... symptoms, if that's not too personal a question?''

"He decided to move the business to Bennington," said Colin.

"No!" said Sunny. "Thirty miles away? There's that Blalock gypsy streak showing up again," she added in a hiss.

"Mother sure thought it was a crisis," Colin said. "She talked him into buying the car instead.''

"The scandals in this family's history..." Sunny marveled.

"Nothing to compare with the Latham family scandal," said Colin. "Maybe you noticed there's no *North* Latham."

"There isn't, is there?" said Sunny, her curiosity aroused. "Why not?"

"I can't tell you," Colin said. "It's too embarrassing. Not the kind of thing a man can tell a woman he...he hardly knows."

"Not even a woman," Sunny said wickedly, "who presented the naked backside of herself to him as a way of saying hello?"

"Sunny!"

"You're blushing! You're actually blushing! Now can you claim we hardly know each other? Tell me about North Latham!"

"No! And I am not blushing. It's sunburn."

"You don't sunburn, not with your complexion. Come on, tell!"

When the caravan scattered to find parking places in Randolph, Colin still hadn't capitulated. He maneuvered the Corvette into a space that couldn't have been more than six inches longer than the car, reached for his door handle, then turned partway toward her. "It's a ten," he said.

"What is?"

"Your backside. Now who's blushing," he purred. But he held her hand as they went to join the family.

By the time they'd set up dozens of lawn chairs, opened coolers to bring out soft drinks and mint tea as well as plastic containers to produce brownies and crisp oatmeal cookies, the parade was under way. The band from South Royalton was followed by floats from day care centers, the dairy industry and Future Farmers of America, Shriners wheeling along the street in their tiny cars and the Randolph High School band playing "Yesterday." Accomplished riders preened on their proud-stepping horses—and then the whole thing came to a halt.

From the near distance came a train whistle and the grinding of wheels along the tracks. All eyes turned to watch the train race through town. "It's like this every year," Aunt Rosamond explained. "We've come to think of it as just another float."

From Randolph they went to Northfield, where a branch of the Blalocks who didn't like crowds barbecued chicken for lunch. "Crowds" didn't extend to family, apparently, because they joined the caravan in the late afternoon to Adamant, where additional assorted Blalocks provided kegs of beer and boiled Maine lobsters. Sunny was afraid to let go of Babe's leash for a second, fearing she might next see him barbecued or boiled. "The parade was wonderful," said Sunny. "And now the fireworks?" She speared a cube of lobster and dipped it into melted butter. "Won't you be exhausted by the time you take me home?"

Colin reached out with a napkin to wipe butter off her chin. His touch sharpened the edge of tension she'd felt building between them throughout the day. A sense of anticipation teased her, warmed her, made her toes curl when her hand brushed his, or when he lifted the heavy weight of hair off her neck to let the late-afternoon breeze cool her heated skin.

"Aunt Sunny," said a little voice. "Can Babe Ruth play with us?"

Aunt Sunny? She gave Colin a startled glance. He affected an active interest in the sunset. "He'd love to," Sunny said, smiling at Kate's younger child, Jessica.

IN MONTPELIER the expanded Blalock forces spread themselves out on blankets to wait for the fireworks. Babe ensconced himself at the center of a clique of Blalock children, and Margaret instructed Colin to share a blanket with

Sunny in an inconspicuous spot toward the back of the group. His mother was wasted in her present occupation; she ought to take over AT&T, or perhaps Iraq.

For once, he didn't mind. That scared him. Too bad he found Sunny so desirable. Desire could lead you into territory best left unexplored. If he could make love to her without caring about her, that would be one thing. But it wasn't his style.

He shifted his shoulder against hers and felt his pulse race. Maybe he could change his style. She was too much like Lisa to take seriously. Not that Lisa was small, red-haired, funny or outrageous, but she knew how she wanted her life to progress, and so did Sunny. When Colin did not choose to progress in the same direction, she chose her life plan over Colin. So would Sunny. They had the hopes and dreams of city girls, the right clothes, the right friends, the right neighborhood...

The fireworks interrupted his train of thought. With the first *boom*, he noticed a small flurry among the family spread out in front of them. The flurry became an uproar as Babe tore wildly through the crowd, upsetting thermoses and plates of food. "Watch the baby!" someone screamed as he mowed past a sleeping infant and vaulted another, looking for Sunny, wanting her to protect him from, as far as he was concerned, a particularly virulent form of thunder.

Panting furiously, he leapt onto her chest, knocking the breath out of her, then dived beneath the blanket where he lay shivering, wriggling and giving out an occasional moan of terror.

"Mmm," said Colin, stunned.

Sunny recovered her breath enough to say, "He always does this. He's terrified of thunder. It's his fatal flaw, or one of them."

"How," said Colin, "do we, ah, calm him down?"

"About all I can do," Sunny said, "is hold him tight until the storm passes."

"I'll hold him tight," said Colin. He rearranged himself and Babe so that Babe, still beneath the blanket, lay firmly crooked under one arm. *And now,* he thought helplessly, *the only thing I want out of life is to put my other arm around Sunny.*

EXPLOSIONS in brilliant colors pounded overhead, reflecting themselves in Colin's eyes. They were beautiful eyes, dynamic eyes. Sunny was certain that Babe still shivered and moaned beneath the blanket, but he'd stopped his frantic wriggling. She couldn't help imagining herself being encircled by Colin's other arm, and then, without any maneuvering on her part, she was.

She relaxed into the warmth of it, cherished the tenderness of it and snuggled up to him. Colin turned his head to gaze at her. His hand slid lightly down her side to rest on her hip, and when she instinctively moved against it, she felt the heat from his skin through the fabric of her dress. It traced a path upward, brushing her breast, then cupped her shoulder, caressing it with a touch as light as an angel's kiss.

As a burst of warmth shot through the center of her body she lifted her face to his, ready to let down her guard completely when a display of color from the heavens lit up his blue eyes. They glimmered at her, knowing, assessing, judging. He was asking her an all-important question, and her body was begging her to say, "Yes." Her eyes closed, her lips parted, and she felt him reach down to cover them with his.

They'd grown hair! Sunny's eyelids flew open. Babe, newly unnerved by the detonation of the American flag into the heavens, had wriggled out from under Colin's arm and leapt between their faces. "My, Grandmother, what a furry mouth you have," she said, sitting up abruptly and picking dog hair off her teeth.

Colin laughed. The mood shattered like the explosion of one more rocket.

————————

7

"HE'S DRAINED," said Sunny. "He played too hard, and he's been through such emotional tension!" She'd just come back to Bev's porch from putting Babe to bed.

"I have, too," said Colin. "I mean, I am, too. Drained."

She smiled at him. "It's been a wonderful day," she said. To her surprise, she meant it, even if she had felt as though she were running for political office.

"There's one exactly like it every year," said Colin.

"I'm glad I was here to have the experience," she said.

"Me, too," said Colin, and gathered her in his arms. His mouth covered hers softly. His breath was sweet, like new-mown grass and strawberries. The shock of discovery made her breathless, and her lips moved against his, opening to him like a blossoming rose. He groaned, and his hands slid down to cup her bottom and lift her off her feet, pulling her tightly against his hardness.

The sensation was exquisite, and wanting more, she parted her legs as though to receive him. She felt his gasp against her mouth as his hands worked her skirt up until they encountered the satiny softness of her panties. They were so hot, those hands. Sunny writhed against their pressure and felt his kiss deepen with a kind of desperation. As though he suddenly realized how little privacy they had, he took a sharp breath and slid his mouth away from hers to bury it under her ear. "Definitely a ten," he murmured, his voice husky, "a ten short, but a ten. Good night, Sunny."

He lifted his head, raised his voice. "Good night, Bev," he added. "Good night, Greg."

Sunny whirled just in time to see a curtain twitch. She was down to earth again, and Colin was gone. She was instantly lonely—and desperately frustrated.

COLIN DROVE HOME through the starry night thinking hard, convertible top down, windscreen off, hoping the suffocating rush of air would cool him down, blast a little oxygen to his brain. He had probably made a mistake today. He'd decided to let down his defenses, leave himself open to whatever Sunny had to give, and he had a hot, edgy feeling that she might have been willing to give a very great deal indeed. Was what she had to give—her delicious little body, her energy, her unquenchable spirit—all he wanted from a woman? What else *could* a man want?

A little depth, maybe? Let's start with the dog. He had to admit she took good care of him, but Babe was just a toy to her, a doll to dress up and take places. *Now, the cottage.* She hadn't abused it, either, but Woodbine Cottage was just a means to an end—a down payment on an apartment in New York. He'd hoped she would fall in love with the cottage. If she did, she might be able to fall in love with him.

Of course, he'd thought Lisa was in love with him. She certainly acted as though she were in love with him. He was just out of the architecture program; she'd just gotten her undergraduate degree from Wellesley. She was smart, she was beautiful, she came from a good Boston family, how could he go wrong with Lisa? So he asked her to marry him, and she set about making plans for their future together.

"We'll live in Boston," Lisa said, her smile soft, her voice firm. "The best neighborhood, darling, for young people just starting out is—"

"After I explore the job options," said Colin, "we'll talk about housing."

"Of course, dear," said Lisa, and went shopping for bridesmaids' dresses.

"You want to run your own business out of a house on the East Latham village green?" she said several months later, no longer smiling. "Where would we go? What would we do? Your family will be all over us! When could I use my sterling?"

"We'd go to bed," said Colin. "We'd make love. I thought that's what marriage was. And why can't my family eat with sterling? You think they're going to steal it?"

That was their next-to-last serious conversation. The last one was brief: "I'll cancel the order for my wedding dress before I'll be a contractor's wife in that nothing town!"

"I'll return the engagement ring before I'll put this tuxedo on one more time!"

That was a long time ago. Now the memory made him smile. He never thought about Lisa anymore, but he did think about the kind of woman he wanted to fall in love with—soon, he hoped. She wouldn't be anything at all like Lisa, so falling in love with Sunny would be a very inefficient use of his limited time and—

The realization of the path his thoughts had taken stunned him. He wasn't anywhere close to thinking about love. So far, Sunny looked just like another Lisa…

His eyes narrowed. There must be something about her he was missing. His family had held back a little with Lisa. With Sunny, they'd been acting like the Welcome Wagon. His mother saw qualities in her that he couldn't, and his mother was one sharp lady. Maybe he would let down his defenses for another day or two.

"HERE. Make yourself useful."

Sunny gazed at the wide paintbrush. "You're going to

let me paint the fence?''

"I'm going to give you an audition," said Colin. "You couldn't do any worse than Norman Fetzer."

"I read an entire book on painting," Sunny told him. "I'll pass this test with flying colors. And I work cheap. Gee, it's nice not to be exiled from my own cottage anymore," she added, sending him a pointed glance. "Why the change of heart?"

"A desperate need for cheap labor. I may hire Norman to do a few things."

"The butcher?" Sunny said, astonished. "You'd let him work for you?"

"Hauling trash or something like that," said Colin. "I'm having a heck of a time putting together a crew to finish this place and the Larribees'. Get that drip." He stood up to look over the top of the fence at the outsides of the palings. "Why am I worrying about a drip? You've sloshed a pint of paint over the fence!"

"Did anybody ever tell you you're hard to work for?" Sunny complained, bending double over the fence to see what he was talking about. "Oh, my gosh," she said hurriedly when she saw the rapidly drying streams of paint.

"Don't lean on the fence!" said Colin. "Look. You've got two white triangles right on your..." He paused, spun away from her, rounded the gate and faced her from the outside of the fence. Sinking down on his haunches, he began to smooth out the drips. "Paint," he ordered her.

She applied her brush to the palings. Through them, he gazed at her, his eyes soft. She tensed up. The brush slowed.

"Sunny, come closer."

Her pulse speeded up. "Why? What have I done now?" She put her face up to the gap between the palings.

"Closer."

Her face rested against the palings. His lips barely met hers, but the light touch sent a drumroll thrumming through the center of her body. He let her go; she gazed at him. Her nose wrinkled.

"How much paint is on my face?" he said calmly.

"A lot."

"As much as you have on yours?"

Her hand shot to her cheek, encountering stickiness. "Into the house," she commanded him, leaping up, "before anybody notices."

In the kitchen their arms tangled together as they scrubbed at each other's faces. "There," said Sunny. "Your mother will never guess we've been spooning in the front yard." She sighed. "There's not a lot of privacy around here, is there?"

"You noticed," Colin commented, still eyeing her with obvious intent.

She dragged her gaze away from his. "How about something cold to drink?" As she took old-fashioned root beer out of the refrigerator, Colin's arms slid around her, molding her waist, then wrapping her tightly. She sank back against him and felt his mouth at her nape, pushing her hair aside to nuzzle her skin. Her breath quickened and she tilted her head, relishing the way his kiss slid across her neck to the squirmy spot beneath her ear.

"What about your house?" she said breathlessly. "Is it more private there?"

She felt his jolt of surprise and wondered if she'd been too aggressive. "Less," he said. The words came out huskily through lips swollen with quick arousal. "I'm the most available—correction, only available—male in town." He hesitated. "I'd like to take you there, but I'm afraid it would make the weekly newspaper."

"What do people do around here, then?" Sunny said, cutting to the chase.

"They get married," Colin said abruptly.

"Oh," Sunny said hurriedly, anxious to get away from this particular topic. "I suppose it figures, I mean..." To her relief, the telephone rang. "Starlight!" she said when she answered it. "How are you and Poppa?"

"Just great, honey," said her mother. "We're moving."

The tingling sensations Colin had aroused in her faded, a familiar feeling of worry taking their place. She turned her back to Colin. "What about Poppa's job?"

"He quit," said Starlight. "So we're going to try house-sitting for a while."

"Dammit," said Sunny, under her breath. "Why'd he quit?"

"You know your father. His boss wanted him to take shortcuts, so he got mad and just walked away. Here he is, honey. Make it fast. We're in a phone booth."

Sunny sighed. "Hi, Poppa." She heard the jangling of coins.

"How's my Sunshine?"

"Fine, just fine. Do you need money, Poppa? I'll send you..."

"We're okay for now," he said. "We don't need much. This house-sitting business is great! They pay you, and you get a free house!"

For a week, Sunny thought, or a month at the most. That seemed to be as far ahead as her parents could think. Swiftly she jotted down the address her father gave her. She'd send them money for rent and deposits when they realized that house-sitting clients eventually came home. It wouldn't be the first time, or the last.

"STARLIGHT?" Colin asked when she was off the phone. A lot of the life had gone out of her, and he wanted to know why.

"My mother." Sunny sighed deeply. "Her real name is Lillian."

"Where are they?"

"Seattle."

"Doing what?" He was so interested that the question popped out of his mouth before he remembered that in his neck of the woods, nosiness was a cardinal sin.

"Starlight plays the guitar and bakes bread and spins wool from fleece she gets directly off sheep. Poppa's in construction," Sunny said.

"Really? What's his name?" What a weird twist. You'd think the first thing she would have told him was that her father was in the same business he was.

"His name is Laurence O'Brien," Sunny said, "but don't bother looking him up. He works for contractors, doing this and that." She paused again, as though she were deciding whether to confide in him. "He quit his job. They're moving. Again."

They sounded like leftover sixties hippies to Colin. "What do you mean by 'this and that'?" he asked, figuring he might as well sin twice.

"Beautiful cabinetry," Sunny said, "and fine repairs to woodwork and floors. You name it, he does it, and he does it well. That's what makes me so mad," she burst out. "He could be working all the time, especially in summer. But no. Once again he gets mad at the boss for not letting him do the job as perfectly as he wants to, and they're off again, in search of truth and beauty."

Colin could recognize a soul mate when one was so vividly described to him. Laurence O'Brien could be the answer to his prayers. "Tell him to come here," he said. "I've got plenty of work for him to do, and he can't do it too perfectly for me." He was excited at the prospect; he'd have a workman he could trust, and the incomplete Sunny would be complete once he met her family.

Sunny's family. He thought he'd done a pretty good job of hiding his surprise. At her worst moments Sunny acted like the sort of spoiled rich kid Lisa was, but apparently she wasn't. His sense of turning an important corner was brought to a screeching halt by Sunny's next words.

"No way," she said flatly. "I've gone through too much to get away from them to bring them back voluntarily."

She hefted a root beer as though it were a shield and marched back to the fence. Colin followed slowly. He couldn't imagine anyone rejecting family the way Sunny had rejected hers. He'd mention the phone call to his mother. It might get her down off her high horse. Sunny had said something about going to New York later in the week. He'd back off a little until she returned, give himself a chance to think about this new side of her.

"ALL FINISHED," said Sunny, surveying her domain—three rooms as beautifully restored as she could ever have dreamed of. "It will be so wonderful not to live out of a suitcase anymore. I bet Bev and Greg have been counting the days. Come on, Babe." He scampered after her as she went out the front door toward the Jeep, still carrying on a one-sided conversation with him. "Let's go to New York. We'll move Claire Lazarus into the fifties and move ourselves out of that apartment."

She let him into the car. "I want you to see where you came from, though. Roots are so important." She got him settled in the carrier and gave him a pat on his plaid tam-o'-shanter. "I wish Colin had come over to say goodbye," she said wistfully.

Vermont basked under a glorious summer sun, but the sky darkened as she sped down the freeway through Massachusetts. In Connecticut the rain began, and thunder rolled as she turned onto the Merritt Parkway. Beside her

Babe panted in terror, scrambling to get out of the carrier and into her arms.

"Calm down, sweetheart," Sunny crooned. She reached a hand over to stroke his head. He scrambled even more vigorously, clawing with his hind legs at the restraining carrier. "I know thunder is difficult for you," Sunny said, switching from sympathetic to calmly objective, "but it won't hurt you. It's not after you. It doesn't even know you're here! You're behaving irrationally, Babe—"

The psychoanalytical approach wasn't working, either. Glimpsing a blue Service Area sign through the deluge, Sunny pulled in, parked the car and slung the carrier around her neck, pinning Babe between herself and the steering wheel. "You'd better hope we don't have a wreck," she muttered, and took to the road again, feeling Babe's shivering diminish as she cuddled him against her chest. "Want to sing?" she asked him hopefully, and burst into "The Rain in Spain."

Musical theater tunes got them down the parkways and into the city. Under still-darkened skies they walked together into the apartment she had shared with Dexter. Sunny felt a sudden coldness, a flattening of the euphoria she'd been in for the last week. That had been her problem with Dexter, his coldness.

There had been a time when he wanted to make love to her, and she'd assumed that marriage would add the warmth, the mutual need and the sharing of experiences that would cause vibrations to hum between them in a way that she recognized was missing in their relationship. But Dexter didn't have any vibrations to hum.

For a moment Sunny thought about Colin, the virility he exuded from every pore and the vibrations that began humming even before they met each other. Not that Dexter wasn't virile, but for him, sex was a way to relax and marriage was a way to share expenses—in short, a home base from which he felt free to seek out women who didn't want as much from him in the way of intimacy as Sunny did.

As for his acquisition of Babe—Dexter saw a cairn terrier in the televised Westminster Dog Show, and without warning, on a day when the divorce was already in the works and Dexter had moved into the second bedroom, a deliveryman arrived with a crate from a fashionable pet shop. In the crate was a tiny, shivering puppy who couldn't have been more than six weeks old.

It had broken Sunny's heart, opening that crate and trying to comfort that little dog. And, of course, once he'd checked "Buy a cairn terrier" off his To Do list, Dexter took little interest in him. He hadn't realized Babe might cut into his free time by needing to be walked and fed. She'd tried to convince herself to stay out of the transaction, walk around the puddles and force Dexter to accept the consequences of his own actions, but she couldn't.

Thank goodness she'd been there to take care of Babe. What would have happened to him when Dexter moved in with Marielle and her allergies? Back to the pet shop? Into another crate to be delivered to yet another person who had decided on a whim that his life would be complete if only there were a cairn terrier in it?

She felt a sudden, fiercely protective feeling for Babe as he looked up at her, his head tilted. She wondered if he was feeling it, too, the coldness of Dexter's memory. "What we need here, Babe," she told him, using her most clinical tone, "is a warmer, more inviting decor. And Colin to rub our tummies," she added.

Babe's tail wagged. Sunny tilted her head, too, staring back at him. What on earth had made her say that? What she needed was her own apartment, decorated to suit her, whether Colin was in it or not!

She sternly threw off her mood. It would be nice to be reunited with her books and CDs, her music system, her art and pottery, even her clothes. She opened the closet doors. "Did you miss me?" she called inside. Trim, short-skirted suits and silk shirts faced beaded evening dresses and jackets across the closet. She eyed the line of three-inch heels. Where was she going to wear those things now? She blinked. She'd wear them when she moved back to the city, of course.

The telephone rang. "Just calling to remind you to be out of the apartment by the fifteenth," said the cool voice of Dexter's lawyer.

As though she needed reminding. "I'll be out on Sunday," she said. And she couldn't wait. The apartment had already drained the sparkle right out of her.

"Where are you moving?"

None of your business. "I don't know yet," Sunny said.

"How's the dog?"

As though he cared! "Babe's growing up to be a perfect little gentleman," she said. "He's housebroken, he fetches, heels and comes when he's called." *Sometimes.*

"Dexter will be pleased to hear that," the lawyer said.

"Why? He never had the slightest interest in Babe's development."

"On the fifteenth, the perfect little gentleman returns to Dexter."

"Ridiculous!" Sunny scooped Babe up and hugged him to her chest.

"If you could ever bring yourself to read the settlement papers all the way through," the lawyer said dryly, "you'd see that the dog conveys with the apartment."

Sunny's eyes widened. "He's not a light fixture," she snapped. "Dexter left him with me and now he's mine. If you cause me any problems I'll call the Society for Animal Rights. We'll see what their lawyer thinks of moving this baby around from parent to parent, as though he were an...an *animal!*"

"He *is* an animal," said the lawyer.

"You know what I mean," Sunny said stiffly. "The clause wouldn't hold up in court. Babe is mine, and that's that."

"Talk to *your* lawyer," said Dexter's lawyer. "He'll confirm what I've told you." He sounded entirely too calm, too sure of himself for Sunny's peace of mind.

She held Babe on her lap while she made a series of calls. She made sure that the final items for Claire's apartment had been delivered and were waiting in one of Claire's many spare bedrooms; she reminded her part-time assistant, Van, to be on hand tomorrow to help.

These details attended to, she walked the unfriendly rooms, singling out items for the packers who would swarm like driver ants through the apartment tomorrow. She ate some depressing-looking things she found in the freezer and got ready for bed. When she had snuggled Babe in beside her, the phone rang. Sunny let it ring, afraid it might be Dexter's lawyer, or worse, Dexter himself. But it was Colin's voice coming from the answering machine. She grabbed for the receiver.

"Colin?" She relaxed, cuddled into the comforter and let his warm voice flow through her to soothe her jangled nerves.

"Is everything okay?"

"Not okay, dreary," she answered, "the weather, the apartment, Babe and me."

"I heard the weather report. Did Babe give you a hard time during the storm?"

"He had a complete breakdown," said Sunny, without mentioning how she had pulled him together again. "Captain Courageous as always." She rubbed the puppy behind his ears, and he burrowed under her arm, wriggling with delight. "He may not be with me through the thunderstorms of his life, though," she intoned in a soap-opera-announcer voice. The thought was so painful she was afraid she'd cry if she didn't ham it up some. "Dexter's lawyer says that when I leave the apartment I lose the dog. After all the work I've put into him. Can you beat that?"

She waited out a brief silence. "Are you going to let Dexter take Babe back?"

Over my dead body. "It's a temporary whim of his," Sunny said. "It won't actually happen." She gathered the puppy into her arms, continuing her conversation over the top of his head. "Don't you think I'm right?"

"I don't know Dexter," said Colin. He hadn't been able to keep himself from calling her, and now he wished he hadn't. Her tone was brittle; she sounded as though she didn't care whether she kept Babe Ruth or lost him. He rubbed a hand over his chin, wishing he could reach out and touch her, caress the brittleness away.

"Consider it a blessing," she told him. "Anyway, I'm not going to give it another thought." She hesitated. "I was going to stay until Sunday to do a little preliminary apartment-hunting, but I'm so depressed it wouldn't be any fun. I'm coming back Saturday morning instead."

His heart leapt. He couldn't help that, either. He wanted her back, even with the rough edges he longed to smooth out. The phrase spilled into his mind from some deep subconscious pool: *She has so much charm. All she needs is TLC.*

"NEAT RAINCOAT," Van commented as the elevator ascended to the lofty heights of the Lazarus apartment.

Babe's bright eyes peered out from under the hood of his red nylon jacket. "He's outgrowing it," Sunny said with a critical glance at the knit cuffs. "We'll buy new clothes while we're here, a tuxedo for the Amons' party, among other things. He needs so little in Vermont," she added. "I'm afraid we've both relaxed our standards."

"Runs naked through the meadows, does he?" Van asked. "Sounds like my kind of place."

"He wears T-shirts from Baby Gap," Sunny said reprovingly. "Come on, let's get this show on the road." Claire would return from the Hamptons this afternoon. Sunny was determined to present her with the finished product, to revel in her delighted shrieks, to accept, eventually, her delightful check.

Van set up the ironing board and pressed each curtain before attaching it with brass clips to a simple brass rod. Sunny tore kraft paper off fuchsia shag area rugs to lay on the bare blond floors. While Babe played in the paper, she unpacked accessories, some of which she'd bought at yard sales for almost nothing, others from specialty shops in SoHo, which had cost the earth. She and Van hung paintings and positioned sculpture from the extensive Lazarus collection. Claire burst in to find them standing in the middle of a perfect room. Screeching with delight, just as Sunny had imagined, she admired the finished product. Sunny had just begun to relax when Claire said, "Now, Sunny…"

This was it, the moment Claire would offer to recommend her to her friends.

"…this looks very cute. It will be such fun for our party."

"I hope you'll enjoy it," Sunny said warmly. "That's a major reward of my job."

"And another reward is other jobs. Right?"

"Right," said Sunny. Claire was taking such a long time about it!

"Before I can give you my unconditional recommendation, I have to see how flexible you are." Claire smiled teasingly.

"I'm afraid I don't understand."

"But you will! Come see what I found!"

Sunny and Van followed Claire to a guest room at the

back of the apartment. "Ta-da!" Claire sang as she flung open the door. "Italian! Original finishes, original upholstery, perfect condition! And it was a steal!"

Sunny stared. The room was stacked with furniture from the twenties and thirties, matched bedroom sets, a white leather sofa, a sideboard and a gigantic dining table lying top down on the bed with chairs upholstered in more white leather stacked on it. "What beautiful furniture," she said, "but it's art deco."

"I know, and that's why I want you to dig in right now and start designing the apartment to go with it! I want everything in black and white," Claire said dreamily.

"I will certainly look forward to doing another job for you," Sunny said untruthfully. "I'm tied up right now with some other things, but…"

"You can't be too tied up to redesign the apartment for me!" Claire exclaimed. "I want it finished in time for the Count's visit in October," she purred at her hapless designer. "We won't have to redo the floors. Just think of that!"

Sunny thought of it. She thought of the clients whose needs she'd pushed aside to finish this design in time for Claire's party. She'd promised the Amons to restore their apartment exactly as it was when they came home to it as a young married couple—in time for their fiftieth wedding anniversary in mid-September. She'd promised the McLaffertys that their considerably less grand apartment would be finished when they returned from their honeymoon in early October. And those were only the big jobs. Other people waited for a few minutes of her attention, a wallpaper, a handwoven rug, an empty corner made beautiful.

The cottage waited, too. Getting it ready to sell was the key to the rest of her life. She couldn't do it all, so what would she choose to do?

"No," said Sunny. "I can't do it by October."

"What if I threw in a little bonus?" said Claire, her voice sharpening.

"I don't need more money." Was that Sunny O'Brien talking? She couldn't say Colin hadn't taught her a few things. As Van gasped, Sunny smiled.

"THE OPERATION was a success, but the patient died," she told Colin when he called again that evening.

"Who died?"

She told him about her day. "Mmm," he said. "So you can't do Claire's job because you have other commitments. Where have I heard that before?"

"There is no similarity whatever between Claire's *utterly* unreasonable demands," Sunny argued, "and my *totally* understandable need for a place to live!" She paused, listening to Colin. "Stop laughing, Colin! I mean it!"

"Have you heard any more from Dexter about Babe?" said Colin.

He had stopped laughing. She wished he hadn't mentioned it. "Of course not," she scoffed. "I'm stuck with him." She gave Babe a bite of smoked salmon.

It surprised her to hear Colin sigh deeply, then change the subject. "Hurry home, Sunny," he said. "Go with me to an auction Sunday."

"That sounds like fun," Sunny agreed. "What are we going to buy?"

"You could use a bench in your mudroom," said Colin, "something to sit on when you take off your snow boots."

Sunny felt better when she hung up. He'd said, "Hurry home." It had a nice ring to it, even if it wasn't accurate. Vermont wasn't home, New York was. And snow boots were a moot point; she'd be long gone before she'd have a need for snow boots. She looked thoughtfully at Babe. "I saw the cutest doggy boots in the *Pampered Pets* catalog," she told him, "and a little snowsuit, bright red."

8

"WE WERE HOME FREE," Colin complained, "and then *you* had to say, 'We can wait until after church to leave. We're only looking for a bench.'" The Corvette shot off down the thruway.

"I couldn't help myself," Sunny said. "Your mother looked so disappointed when you said we had to leave right after breakfast."

"She's got that look down to a science," Colin grumbled.

"Well, ex*cuse* me," said Sunny. "I was trying to be thoughtful of her feelings."

"The high point of my morning was seeing my father hooked into going to church," said Colin, a vengeful smile curving his lips. "Your sympathetic moment came too late for him to get out of it."

"I'm glad I achieved something," Sunny said haughtily. She gazed at the countryside they whizzed past. Large branching wildflowers with deep blue blossoms had joined the daisies along the roadside. The color scheme was very appealing. Maybe she should add something indigo-flowered to her butter-yellow-and-white bedroom. She needed to take a close look at her budget, though. She'd just dispatched a large check to her parents—and turned down a big job.

"Sunny…" said Colin.

The word was like a kiss. It sent a little shiver of desire straight down through the center of her body. She turned to see his face, the way his eyes would have softened and his lips parted. What she saw was Babe's nose and wiry brindle bangs. "We've got to do something different with this dog," she complained.

Colin made a small, impatient sound. "Babe's fine," he said. "Just look around him. I was trying to tell you something."

"I'm sorry," she said politely. "What?"

"I was trying to tell you I wasn't really mad."

The caress was back in his voice. Drenched with pleasure, Sunny wanted to reach out for him. Suddenly frightened by the sure and certain knowledge of what she ultimately wanted, she said, "I knew you wouldn't be. You like seeing your mother happy."

COLIN'S EYES narrowed, and he withdrew the hand he'd been sliding across the seat of the car. He'd hoped to see her soften, lose her crisp, abrupt edge, let him spend the afternoon courting her in the old-fashioned way, with his eyes, his voice and his touch. But how could you court a woman who said, at a tender moment, "We've got to do something different with this dog"?

He sighed. When she'd swept into the driveway yesterday afternoon and barreled into the cottage to greet him with a hug and a kiss and an avalanche of talk, every molecule of his body had risen to meet her. So much for holding back. He'd felt himself blushing, for God's sake, like a lovesick teenager! He was dying to make love to her, but he had to feel closer to her first. Sex was something you built up to, and virtually impossible to do with a woman who'd just said, "We've got to do something different with this dog"!

He tried again. "Yes, I like to see Mother happy. That seems to be my job. Dad and Marty do whatever they want, she gets all stirred up, and I'm supposed to make everything all right."

"You're the good son," said Sunny. "It's obvious your brother inherited your dad's rebellious streak. It's a pain, isn't it?" she went on. "Feeling responsible, I mean? I had Claire in the palm of my hand. Then I started thinking about the promises I'd made to the Amons and the Mc-Laffertys and fourteen other clients, and I blew it with Claire. Was that silly of me?" She leaned forward, by-passing Babe's wet brown nose.

"I don't think so," said Colin. He felt off balance again. He'd hoped, had actually halfway decided, that she'd turned down the latest Lazarus whim because she wanted to come back to Vermont, to the cottage, to him, even if the spiny part of her wouldn't admit it. Now she was talking about a mob of additional clients. The prospect of making love, which had taken a shy step forward, took two steps back.

"I hope not," said Sunny. "I decided I'd be better off professionally by meeting my obligations than I would with Claire's recommendation."

It was time to bring up a touchy subject. "Why don't you feel an obligation to your parents?" He couldn't get the prospect of Laurence O'Brien working for him off his mind.

She hesitated for a moment, then said, "Why should I? They didn't feel obligated to me. They made sure I didn't starve, and that was it. I had to register myself for kindergarten."

He wanted to know what had run through her mind during that brief silence, but the bright striped auction tents loomed up ahead. The bench he'd seen listed in the newspaper had already sold, but Sunny's attention was gripped by a pair of chairs, some Shaker nightstands and a thirties-style ottoman—she called it a "pouf"—a huge celery green thing with fringe that she said was exactly what she needed for the Amons' living room. She reached for the numbered card the auctioneer's assistant had given Colin.

"I'll bid," he said, keeping a tight grip on the card.

"Why can't I bid?"

He could feel her competitive juices running high. "It's a well-known fact that New Yorkers drive prices up. I'm a local. I'll bid."

"Do we drive the prices up? Or do you drive them up to see how much we're willing to pay?" She balled up her hands into fists, ready to start swinging.

"A little of both," Colin said. Her carroty red hair curled crazily around her face and brushed her shoulders, which the summer sun had turned pale gold beneath their splash of freckles. Her long sundress was pretty and old-fashioned, printed with daisies like her bathroom wallpaper. His irritation vanished. He wanted to slide his hands around her waist, lift her high off her feet and let her swing—at an altitude at which she couldn't do any harm. There was so much energy in that little body. He was dying to have it all, to use it up making love with her, except for the difficulty he was having getting close enough to introduce the subject. It was like…

"You don't want that pouf," he heard Sunny confiding to the man on her right. "It's not that old, and it probably has fleas." She hissed the last word.

…it was like she'd fallen down and scraped her heart, the way Scooter fell down and scraped his knees, but it sounded as though Sunny didn't have a mother like Belinda to dry the tears and clean the scrape with something that didn't hurt, and put on a bandage that would be the envy of the neighborhood. She'd had to take care of the scrape herself. Scar tissue had formed, unresilient and impenetrable, and that was what you encountered first when you tried to reach her heart. What he had to know was whether the scar tissue went all the way through, or whether beneath it lay a new, tender and yielding heart that was capable of the kind of love he had to have from a woman—a love that put him first, not an opportunistic love like Lisa's.

His thoughts faded as he listened to the highly illogical argument she was carrying on single-handedly about her right to bid. Babe Ruth in his baby-sized T-shirt sat on her lap looking at him with a disgruntled expression similar to the one Sunny was wearing. She couldn't give in without a fight, but when the chairs she wanted reached the auctioneer's block, Colin noticed that she kept her mouth tightly shut.

When he got the chairs, she reached over to squeeze his hand. That simple touch, added to the thoughts that already crowded his mind, caused a sudden quickening below his belt. When he got the ottoman, she grabbed his entire arm, crushing it to her. "The Amons will be amazed," she said. "That pouf could have been the one in their living room fifty years ago!"

"Glad to help," he said, trying desperately to think about icy mountain streams, falling down on skis and his last trip to the dentist instead of the pressure of her small, perfect breasts against his arm.

"Why didn't you bid higher on the little tables?" she said accusingly, not an hour later.

"The price was already too high," Colin said, almost relieved that she was back to arguing. "It's fairly obvious by now I'm bidding for you," he pointed out.

"I liked them."

"We'll find more—at lower prices," Colin said. His mother had about six of them in the attic. She'd give two to Sunny.

"We'd better," said Sunny. "I had my heart set on them."

Colin smiled. "Time to go, wheeler-dealer. I've got a picnic in the car."

"A picnic! How wonderful!" The tables forgotten, she gave him a smile that reduced his muscles to jelly. He picked up their lawn chairs, settled matters with the auctioneer and ushered Sunny and Babe back into the Corvette. He was about to face his most important test of the day, and he felt primed to fail.

"IT'S ABSOLUTELY beautiful," Sunny breathed. She stood in the center of a little clearing surrounded by woods, listening to the tinkle of a small stream as it wove its way down the hillside. The ground was padded with dry pine needles, and rays of sunlight slid down through the surrounding trees to make a flame-stitch design of light and shadow. "It's straight out of a storybook. How did you find this place?"

"It's part of the cross-country ski trail," Colin said.

Sunny helped him spread a quilt over the pine needles. Babe peered over the bank into the stream, thought better of it and returned to peer into the picnic basket, which seemed more promising. Nervous about losing him in the wilds, Sunny had him on a leash that let out like a tape measure when she released the catch.

Colin opened the cooler, took out a bottle of wine and opened it with swift competence. "Wine?" Sunny said. "When we're working?"

Dammit, I'm trying to seduce you! Work is easier! "I brought sparkling water, too, if you'd rather," he said, feeling edgy.

"I was just teasing you," she protested. She settled herself on the quilt, her dress billowing out around her, and eyed the picnic basket as hopefully as Babe did.

He poured wine into plastic cups and pulled out the rest of the contents of the cooler—a plate of cold ham, a container of pasta salad, another of coleslaw. The basket held corn muffins and brownies, oatmeal cookies and tangerines, and a strangely dry-looking cookie that Sunny eyed dubiously. "What are those?" she said.

"Dog biscuits," said Colin. "Homemade. One of Fiona's specialties."

Sunny admired them. Colin had brought a jar of water for Babe, too, and a plastic bowl. "You thought of everything," she complimented him. She wouldn't mention the bottle of water she carried for Babe in her huge straw handbag along with a bag of admittedly grocery-store dog biscuits, not when Colin had been so thoughtful of Babe's comfort. "You don't have a dog, do you?" she asked him.

"I have a tomcat," said Colin.

"A cat!" said Sunny. "And you've never mentioned him?"

"Muffler is not the kind of cat you mention," Colin said cryptically.

"I want to meet him sometime," said Sunny. "Not when Babe's with me, though." She sighed, then took a bite of pasta salad directly from the container and chewed for a minute. "I talk to him and talk to him, but he's *unusually* unresponsive about this cat-chasing business."

"I'd like to see Babe's reaction to Muffler," Colin said. "We'll have to get them together sometime soon." He smiled at her.

The smile, combined with the way his gaze trailed over her face and throat, made Sunny realize that in this forest glade they were at last alone. The thought spread through her body, heating her blood, making her feel heavy and swollen at her womanly center. The sense of urgency she felt inside unnerved her. Her hands trembled a little as she filled a plate for Colin, and then one for herself. "I was thinking again this morning," she said, in an effort to distract herself, "how comfortable you are around your family."

"Does that bother you?" said Colin. It had bothered Lisa—when she realized that he was so comfortable around his family he wanted to stay around them.

"Oh, no," Sunny said. "It makes me jealous. This is great coleslaw. Did your mother make it?"

"Mmm," Colin said, trying not to sound impatient. "You said jealous?" He wanted to know what she meant, but more than that, he wanted her to gaze at him with the look he'd seen earlier in her eyes, a look of anticipation, expectation, promise. He did not want to talk about coleslaw!

"I wasn't comfortable with my parents," Sunny said. "I never knew what they were going to do next. When my father would take a notion to move on, we'd pack ourselves into whatever sort of car he was driving at the moment and take off. I never knew where I was going to sleep, or whether the car would break down and we'd have to spend all our money repairing it."

His parents weren't rich, but there had never been the slightest possibility that they would run totally out of money. "If it did break down, what did you do?"

"We slept outside a few times, and once we just settled in the town where the car fell apart." She gave him a sparkling smile.

She was her usual blithe self, but Colin felt suddenly angry at these people. How could anybody do that to a kid? Maybe some kids thrived on adventure, the way Sunny's parents seemed to thrive on it themselves, but why couldn't they see that their little girl didn't feel the same way?

"I guess," Sunny said, "you can see how why I'm so hooked on having a permanent home. After I started working, the minute I scraped enough money together I rented an apartment in Chelsea. Two hundred twenty-five square

feet all my own. I stayed there, too, saving money while
my fortunes grew, until I..." Her expression sharpened.
"You know what, Colin? Maybe the only reason I married
Dexter was that together we could afford to buy! Thirty-
five percent down," she marveled. "Can you imagine?"

Colin didn't want to talk about urban real estate, either,
and sure didn't want to think about Sunny married to Dexter. He wanted to tell her that he finally saw why she
needed him to restore the cottage, finally understood why
she watched every penny, although she seemed to have
plenty of money by most people's standards. His heart was
racing. She was, at last, opening up to him. If only he could
get her to stop talking about that damned apartment she
would buy in New York!

Of course, if she stopped talking about it, or started talking about staying in the cottage, his longing to cover her
body with his would go out of control. He was having to
keep a tight rein on himself as it was.

"Have a brownie," he suggested.

"Thank you." She bit into the chocolate frosting with
small, pearly teeth. "Um, yummy," she murmured, licking
chocolate off her lips with the tip of her tongue. Colin's
eyes followed the path of that small pink tongue, imagining...

When he couldn't stand it anymore, he leaned over and
licked the last scrap of chocolate from the corner of her
mouth. He felt her shiver, felt her jolt of uncertainty and
moved closer, sliding his lips across hers. She relaxed
against him, letting the kiss happen, kissing him back,
opening her mouth to him and giving him its sweetness to
savor.

A surge of desire threatened to carry him away. He
wanted to take it slowly, make her want him as much as
he wanted her, but every nerve in his body screamed at him
to take her now, while he could. It had been a long time,

such a long time. He fought down his need, concentrating on exploring this minute part of her. Her lips grew softer, swollen and moist. When she moved against him, he pulled her down to the sun-warmed quilt so that her breasts rested against his chest, her hair fell in a cascade around his head and her delicious, chocolate-scented mouth was above his. His hands tightened in the waterfall of red-gold curls, pulling her closer as the kiss deepened.

SHE FLOATED in a pool of sensation, clinging to his mouth as it slid away. His teeth bit lightly into her earlobes, his tongue darted lightly into her ears. Flames licked at her center and she shuddered, whispering his name, as his mouth slid down to the hollow of her throat, to the sensitive pathway to her breasts.

"Was that a 'no'?" he whispered.

"It was a 'don't stop now,'" she murmured.

His hands reached for the zipper at the back of her dress. The dress slipped off her shoulders and her bare breasts fell free. She turned away, sinking into the sun-warmed quilt, and pressed them into the heat of his hands as he kissed her down the length of her spine. He paused at the small of her back, then let his mouth slide down to the last vertebrae.

The ache of pure pleasure wrung a moan from her throat. Her nipples were hard, her breasts full and aching, and desire seared her as the pressure of his kisses deepened against her skin. She was never so aware of her smallness as when he effortlessly turned her back to him and took her nipple between his lips, teasing it with his tongue. She arched her body, moving it into his searching mouth, and he groaned as he took it, then the other, kissing, nibbling, licking each one into a tightly wound spring of pure sensation.

Leaving her wanting more, his kisses slipped down to

seek the tender, moist, pulsing heart of her womanhood with that warm mouth, that sweet-rough darting tongue. His skillful hands pulled the dress farther down from her body until she was almost naked in the late afternoon light, and when they reached the barrier of her panties they tugged gently until the barrier was crossed. She reached for him, encouraged him, arched herself toward him, demanded the delicate probing, thrusting.

She was losing control, losing her hold on reality. Her knees were so much cotton candy, her body a writhing, demanding vessel that seemed to have a life of its own. She struggled for the last shards of her reason. Was this the right thing to do? Was it right for Colin?

"I need to ask you…" she said, gasping for breath.

"Oh, God, not now," he groaned.

"I want to tell you…"

Her questions didn't seem to matter anymore. She could keep her body at bay no longer. "I want to tell you that your hair is like silk, and it tickles when you kiss my back, and your mouth is so soft, oh, Colin, oh…"

She thrust toward him and screamed as sensation took over to leave sensibility behind in the slick pine needles, the soft cotton of their bed, the truth of their lives.

HER BODY SOUGHT his out, more and more of it, light as a golden leaf as it lay on his. There was no need to hide his arousal any longer. She must know how desperately, how urgently he desired her. It was agony to let her go long enough to shed his clothes, agony to attack the foil packet with shaking fingers, but he wanted to take care of her, to protect her. At last ready for her, he pulled her over to straddle him and his arousal found the wetness between her legs.

Something made him glance up. Sunny's eyes were closed, her light lashes feathered across her cheeks, where a smattering of new freckles made her look even younger and more vulnerable than she usually did. Babe Ruth lay sleeping on a bed of pine needles, his little body splayed out with his legs behind him. Around Sunny's wrist was the loop of the leash. Colin smiled shakily. If she didn't love the dog, at least she felt responsible for him. Any doubts he might have had vanished.

HE PUSHED against her, hot and hard, and she cried out again as waves rocked her into a dreamworld of pure delight. He was swiftly inside her, and she entered another world, not a dream but a world they shared, one in which she sought to give him the rapture he had given her. He seemed enormous, and she so small. How could she feel so perfectly filled? His thrusts grew frantic, and brought her only pleasure. She pushed back, and his arms crushed her to him as the rhythm of their mad dance quickened. This was for him. It was his turn. Surely everything she did now was for him. Her intensifying desire shocked her, but only for a moment, and then she gave in to it completely and let herself cry out in harmony with his last thrust, his groan, his desperate clinging to her, and finally, blessedly, the sensation of rocketing skyward with him.

She spiraled slowly downward and finally settled, heavy and sated, to earth again. Hot and wet, they clung together. At last he slid her across his sweat-slick chest to lie beside him on the quilt, and Sunny looked up to the benevolence of the late sun and the faint crescent of a moon already starting its arc across the sky.

She was the first to speak. "Well," she said, hearing a voice that wasn't quite her own, "this aspect of our relationship is promising."

His soft laugh was like a new and different caress. "That was just a promise?" he said. "The real thing is still to come?"

"Don't tease me," she said severely. "I'm exhausted."

"I wouldn't want to lift a bathtub myself right now," said Colin, kissing the tip of her nose.

His laugh had awakened Babe Ruth. He came to join them, burrowing between them, wanting to be petted. Colin dropped a hand to his head and complied, digging in deep behind the dog's ears with his large, powerful fingers in the way that made Babe wriggle with delight. With the other hand he fingered her wrist. "That's a new twist," he said. "I never thought I'd make love with a woman who was holding a leash. A whip, maybe…"

"You didn't seem to need a whip," Sunny pointed out.

"No." He smiled at her, a smile that faded slowly. "I never knew I could want anything that much," he said.

"Me, either," she said. She let her mind scan her life with Dexter, briefly, not wanting to linger on it. She remembered their brief physical encounters, businesslike, textbook, both of them technically at peace for the moment, but Sunny was always aware of something missing, something warm, something nourishing that had never been there in Dexter's lovemaking.

Colin was as nourishing as the Good Humor man. She felt the need for another course, a little something sweet to top off the satiating meal. Colin was quiet, too quiet, his mouth raking a trail from her earlobe to her stomach, from her stomach to her…

"Did you bring more of those—"

"I've kept my pockets stuffed with them since the day I saw you in the mirror," he murmured into the soft brush of red-blond curls he had just kissed his way into.

"Good thinking," said Sunny, and gave herself over completely to dessert.

"I GUESS WE HAVE TO go home," she sighed some time later.

"Any regrets?"

Sunny turned to gaze at him. "Aren't those supposed to happen in the morning?" she asked him, and dropped her sundress over her head.

"Let me know in the morning," he said. He zipped her dress, gave her a last light kiss on the back of her neck and grabbed his trousers. In his haste, he'd flopped them over her huge straw handbag, which came with them, upside down. The entire contents spilled out on the quilt, and he eyed her arsenal with amazement.

The usual female stuff, plus a jar of water, a plastic storage bag of dog biscuits, another of dog food, two dog bowls, a second leash, an extremely small T-shirt and a rubber hot dog. "You, ah, were prepared after all," he commented.

"I didn't want you to know after you'd been so thoughtful of Babe," she said.

She'd never know how good it made him feel to see the evidence of her sense of responsibility for Babe Ruth laid out on the quilt like exhibits A to Z. Never? Maybe he'd have a chance to tell her someday soon.

9

"YOO-HOO," called Margaret Blalock.

"Oh, no," Sunny muttered, dusting at her skirt. "What do I look like?"

"You look like a woman who's just made love," said Colin. "Hello, Mother," he added as Margaret bustled out to the car. He opened the door for Sunny and Babe, then lifted the cooler and picnic basket out of the back seat.

"I was hoping to catch you two coming home," said Mrs. Blalock, smiling at Sunny. "Will you come to dinner? I've made an enormous pot roast."

Sunny looked a question mark at Colin. He responded with an uplifted eyebrow. Sunny picked Babe up. "Do we have time to change clothes?"

"We won't eat for another half hour," Mrs. Blalock reassured her. She gave her son a glance fraught with meaning. "Colin will come with us."

Colin had been indulging in a daydream of changing Sunny's clothes from the skin out, giving her a cool bath and exploring every inch of her with a soapy washcloth before zipping her into another soft, long sundress. He saw her longing backward glance as she fled into the cottage. Had she had the same idea? Feeling thwarted, he followed his mother into the roast-scented kitchen. Aunt Rosamond waited at the kitchen table. Colin kissed her cheek, went to the refrigerator and popped the cap off a beer.

"Well?" said Margaret.

"Well what?" said Colin. He took the peanut butter

cookie his mother handed him and bit out a big chunk. Crumbs fell to the floor. Aunt Rosamond scooped them up with a paper towel, then went back to gazing at him eagerly.

"Did anything happen this afternoon you'd like to tell us about?" his mother persisted. To emphasize her point, she extracted a pine needle from Colin's hair.

"No," he said.

"I'm not prying into your private life," Margaret said. "I just wondered, as any mother would, if you had a successful day."

"Okay," Colin sighed, "I'll tell you." Both women leaned forward.

"We bought an ottoman. Horrible green thing. Thank God it's going to New York into an apartment she's decorating. And a pair of chairs. Great chairs. Hepplewhite, original finish, need gluing, new cushions..."

"Colin!" his mother interrupted. "I already know all that. Rose Carter was at the auction. *Everyone's* talking about the ottoman," she said reprovingly.

"How about the chairs?" Colin asked, raising his eyebrows.

"You got a good buy on the chairs," his mother admitted. "Thank goodness you didn't get the side tables, because I've brought the best two down from the attic. Sunny may have those after you reglue them and restore the finish. Speaking of Sunny, what I really wondered, as you know quite well...."

His jaw firmed. "I like Sunny very much, and I enjoy being with her. I think she feels the same way about me. But I've already told you, Sunny plans to sell the cottage and use her profits to buy an apartment in the city. We haven't talked about a change in her plans."

"If she sells the cottage," Margaret said, "she can move

into…she can move somewhere else. All you have to do is talk her out of going back to New York.''

"Romance her out of it," Aunt Rosamond said dreamily.

"Even if she did go back to New York," said Margaret, carrying on her one-sided argument, "it wouldn't be the end of the world. People have commuter marriages these days."

"You didn't suggest a commuter marriage with Lisa," Colin blurted out, too shocked by her suggestion to point out that they hadn't been discussing marriage.

"You weren't in love with Lisa," Margaret said.

"I'm not…" Colin began, then thought of a new strategy. "Or I could move to New York. Do restoration work for decorators. I'd probably make more money than I do here." As soon as the words were out of his mouth, he wondered if he could, in fact, do that. He wondered if he was, in fact, in love with Sunny. He didn't have time for any more wondering. His statement had galvanized his two inquisitors.

"Leave Vermont?" Aunt Rosamond gasped.

"I feel that Blalock gypsy streak coming out in me," Colin said, quoting Sunny.

"Let's not go overboard, dear," Margaret Blalock said nervously. "Let's concentrate on keeping Sunny here." She smiled encouragingly.

"Maybe we ought to let her go her own way," Colin said, enjoying the role of devil's advocate. "How do we know what she'd be like in the long run?" He frowned. "I feel better about her attitude toward the dog, but I'm still bothered by her attitude toward her parents." If that didn't cause his mother to take a step back for another look at Sunny, nothing would.

"I've always known she was crazy about Babe Ruth," his mother said, "but what's this about her…"

A soft knock sounded at the door, accompanied by a hideous scratching sound.

"The kitchen door," Aunt Rosamond breathed.

"She's acting like family," said Mrs. Blalock fondly, "and I do believe that little love of hers is asking to be let in, too!"

He was clawing the paint off the back door! Colin couldn't believe his mother would tolerate it! And then Sunny was among them, a small flurry of blue denim and red plaid sweater, her Fourth of July outfit. Clarabelle the cat leaped to the top of the refrigerator as Babe, also wearing blue denim, danced from one person to the other. Martin Senior came in from the sitting room, where Colin suspected he'd been jailed by the women until they'd had time to pump him for information.

The serene, orderly kitchen came alive. *Damn!* Colin thought. *If only she'd stop dressing up that dog!*

DURING DINNER, Kate called. "Sunny," said Margaret, "can you talk to her?"

"Sure." Sunny put down a forkful of roasted potato and went to the kitchen phone. "Kate? Hi."

Colin listened, frustrated when all he could hear were delighted sounds from Sunny. When she came back to the dining room, she looked delighted, too, her eyes shining like green Christmas lights.

"Kate wants to redo her living room now that her kids are big enough to behave themselves," she said. "She asked me to help her."

"How nice," purred Mrs. Blalock.

"Kate loves pretty things," seconded Rosamond.

"No more so than the other girls," said Margaret, "or their friends."

Colin saw the handwriting on the wall. His mother actually thought she could turn Sunny into a southern Vermont decorator. He looked toward his father, hoping for a little manly sympathy and understanding, but all he got was a bland smile.

THE ENTIRE village center of West Latham saw the moving van arrive with Sunny's possessions. Prodded by his mother's phone call to the Larribees' house, where he was working, Colin left the job and came over to see if she needed help unpacking. He found her in the kitchen with Babe Ruth. They both stared at the top of a sealed carton, Babe with his front paws resting on the lid. Even in the privacy of his home, Babe wore a red-striped T-shirt.

"I can't open the box that has the box opener in it," Sunny said glumly. "See how carefully I labeled it? Box opener and tools, right there, but it never occurred to me how I was going to open it. I guess I thought I'd use a knife, or some scissors. They," she gestured toward another carton, "are in that box. And you and your crew are so neat! You'd think there'd be a screwdriver around, or a spatula. I've been working at it with a nail file..." She looked hopefully at Colin.

"No need to fear," he murmured, "Dudley Doright is here." He tugged a razor-sharp opener out of his pocket and ripped open the lid of the first box. Babe promptly fell in. "Here's your ripper," he said. "Go for it."

He watched her open a box and decided she had adequate ripper skills. She looked wonderful in the late-morning light, her hair all in a tumble and her pink shirt turning her skin to butterscotch flecked with bits of pecan. Her light blue jeans fit her small, curving figure tightly. She looked edible; he wanted to devour her in one satisfying bite. Or was it possible he wanted to savor her in small bites, over many decades? He leaned over to give her a kiss.

Her lips melted over his, soft and smooth, mint-scented. The familiar quickening in his loins made him want to toss everything aside—the box opener, the task at hand, the Larribee job, his future—to make room in his arms and in his heart for nothing but her. His hands slid down her back, smoothed over her rounded bottom. Unaccountably, he felt her slipping away from him. She ripped open a box with a gesture that made her thoroughly unkissable. He gave up on the notion of kissing and savagely ripped open a box himself.

She lifted a ceramic bowl from the carton. "Bev's pots survived the trip." She reached up on tiptoe to position it on the shelf Colin had installed above the kitchen fireplace. Without a ladder, she was half an arm's length from reaching the shelf.

He moved up behind her, took the bowl from her hands and put it on the shelf, letting his hands rest at her waist for a moment when he had finished. How could so much sexuality exude from so small a person? He kissed her neck, felt her shiver and lean into him before she fluttered away like a frightened moth.

She had the unpacking under control. It was time for him to get back to the Larribees' place, but he couldn't seem to get his legs moving toward the door. Busily she produced more pots and bowls from labeled boxes, glancing up occasionally to see what Colin was pulling out of the boxes he'd opened. Babe pranced happily through the wrappings, scattering foam pills from one end of the kitchen to the other. "Don't open that one," she said suddenly.

"All right." Colin moved on to the next box, wondering if he'd narrowly missed the chance to run his hands through silken nightgowns, lacy panties.

"It's my formal china. I won't need it here. I have a set of Bev's wonderful pottery. And those two wardrobe boxes. Those are suits and party dresses. They go to the back of the storage closet for now."

The erotic thoughts playing havoc with Colin's libido

cooled; he was surprised at the way his heart sank. A memory ran through his mind:

"What will I do with my sterling?"

"I think enough of my parents to let them eat with the sterling."

They unpacked silently for a while, except for his questions about where to put things and Sunny's quick responses. At least she'd been thinking about it. Late in the afternoon the job was finished and the packing materials put in order for the village's perfectionist refuse collector. Colin took them out to the street and returned to the kitchen where Sunny stared at the filled cupboards.

"Amazing how it all fits," she said.

Colin glanced at her surreptitiously, imagining he'd heard tears in her voice.

Her eyes were gleaming emeralds. "It looks like I've been collecting things for the cottage without realizing it."

Hope leaped in his heart.

"This place will sell in a New York minute," she said with relish.

Despondent, Colin took her to Aunt Rosamond's for dinner, where Sunny ate two pieces of rhubarb pie.

THE COMMERCIAL STATEMENT that tripped so blithely from her tongue was entirely different from the thought that shocked her as she watched her possessions settling into Woodbine Cottage: *It's as though I'm supposed to live here.* She'd found the idea so upsetting that all she could do was revert to the mantra she'd been chanting since the day she met Colin: *Fix the cottage, sell the cottage, buy an apartment, move back to New York, make more money, be secure for life...*

She could hardly remember thinking of Colin as a summer fling. It frightened her to realize how much more he had come to mean to her. There was no denying the physical attraction between them, but for brief moments she could deny the sense of security she felt with him, the warmth that exuded from him to surround her, the strange incompleteness she felt when he wasn't around. Then would come a day like today, when she couldn't deny any of those feelings.

But she didn't want him to think she'd changed her plans for the future. In Colin's office, Sex and Love were filed together. The file was labeled Marriage. He was the lover she'd always dreamed of having, but if she went on making love with him and then left to pursue her carved-in-stone agenda, what would it cost him?

It was then, while outwardly she chattered on and inwardly she agonized over what to do about Colin, that she accepted a second piece of Aunt Rosamond's prizewinning rhubarb pie. If she didn't watch it, she'd end up a size four.

"And now," Margaret said after Sunny had wolfed down the pie, "Rosamond will play a piece for us on the organ. She's been working on 'Lady of Spain,'" she confided.

With obvious reluctance, Rosamond sat down at the organ in the parlor. What she did to "Lady of Spain" was, Sunny thought nostalgically, *excremental.* When it was over, she led the applause.

"YOU'VE BEEN AN ANGEL and I'm certainly not hurrying you," said Sunny, "but when do you think the cottage will be finished?"

"Might be a little longer than I thought," said Colin. He was holding down the pedestal sink in the guest bathroom while the plumber wrestled with some pipes beneath it. "It needs a little more support down cellar. We were okay until Dad talked you into this tub."

Unintelligible grunts came from beneath the sink. Colin worked with the most amazing people, a literary plasterer and a convict plumber who got along just fine with the rest of the crew, some of whom descended from generations of fine craftsmen. He tied them together with a single purpose: Do the job right.

Her father, Sunny thought uncomfortably, would fit in just fine.

They eyed the massive cast-iron tub, Colin with malevolence, Sunny with affection. "Okay," she said, sighing, "I won't call a real estate agent yet. If you could give me a rough date, though…"

She wandered back to the work area she'd established in one corner of her bedroom. It wasn't that she wanted to put the house on the market, really, but after a morning like this one, working on the Amon apartment by telephone, having to have samples mailed to her and pictures of furnishings sent by Federal Express—it was getting to be a chore.

It was affecting her business. Her business was interior design, her clients were in New York, and she needed to live where those clients with their endless phone calls lived, where the fabrics and furniture and wall coverings and lighting fixtures that would make them happy were to be found, or she would one day go mad trying to choose a pair of bedroom lamps from a pile of fuzzy faxed pictures.

She stood, wrapping her arms around herself. Who was she kidding? She had to sell the cottage and get out of this place before she became unable to make a sensible decision about her life.

It might already be too late. She had somehow fallen in love with Colin.

How could she have let it happen? A long-term relationship would never work. If she stayed here with him, she'd embrace country life as though it were a new decorating project, and when she'd seen it all and done it all, she'd get bored and regret her choice. Wouldn't she? Wasn't that the sort of person she really was?

"Sunny." Colin popped his head in the door. "Can we talk tile?"

"Sure," said Sunny, her doubts fading to the dangerous level at which she was able to imagine Colin in the next room, or in the same room, all the rest of her life.

An hour later they were still arguing about tile. "Look," Colin said finally, "let's drop it for now. Later this afternoon we'll run over to my house and I'll show you how I did a bathroom there. If you don't like it, we'll do it your way."

"Fair enough," said Sunny, who had only begun to warm to the fight. "You're taking me to your house?" she said in sudden surprise.

"About time, don't you think?" He hesitated. "We'll take Babe with us. It's about time for him to meet Muffler."

About time? Sunny's worry deepened.

"Showing you how I did the tile in my bathroom is better than trying to describe it to you," said Colin. Babe explored the house while Colin led Sunny up the stairs. He seemed nervous. Had he forgotten to pick up his underwear and towels? She felt nervous, too, but not about underwear and towels. She imagined curtains twitching all the way around the village green as disappointed matchmakers checked out the woman they'd heard Colin was walking out with. She followed him into a bathroom that was very clean and relatively neat, and examined the tile.

"Okay," she said, "we'll do it your way."

Colin's eyes widened, so blue they dazzled her. "Did I hear you right?" he said. "Did I hear you say to do it my way?"

"Like you said, I needed to see it. Now I have."

"You don't mind if I sit down," said Colin, sinking to the toilet seat. "This is such a shock. Do you carry spirits of ammonia in that giant bag of yours?"

"Oh, Colin, you know I always do what you say to do when it comes to the cottage." Sunny paused. From the floor below came the unmistakable toenail-clicking sounds of one animal chasing another. "We have to rescue Muffler!" she cried.

As she pounded toward the stairs, Sunny caught a glimpse of a big, masculine campaign bed, a spartan white coverlet and antique dressers, but the emergency on the floor below outweighed even her curiosity about Colin's bedroom. Two shapes whizzed past the foot of the maple staircase, one brindle, one tabby gray. "Babe, stop it," she shouted. "Don't chase the…" As the pair circled the downstairs and flew by her again, she did a double take. "That's odd," she said, turning to Colin. "It almost looked as though Muffler was chasing…Babe!" she screamed when she heard the high, sharp barks of Babe in terror.

Racing to the rescue, she found Babe in the center of a long harvest table in the kitchen, his tail tucked between his legs, shrieking down a warning at the biggest, ugliest, most disreputable-looking cat she'd ever seen.

It was a huge gray tabby, with one of his ears mostly missing and a crooked tail, as though it had been broken. One eye was inoperative; the other sized her up with a hard yellow gaze. If Babe attacked this cat, she'd be identifying his little body in the morgue. Sunny scooped him into her arms, where he immediately began to bark like a victor. "Shh," she said crossly. "You're all bluster." Embarrassed, he quieted down.

"Muffler, where's your sense of hospitality?" said Colin, picking the cat up. A sound like a subway train rumbling beneath a sidewalk came from the very depths of the animal.

"I see why you named him Muffler," she said faintly. "He needs a new one."

Colin looked at the cat as though he were seeing him afresh. "I named him Muffler because of the way he drapes himself around my neck," he said.

"He could swallow Babe in one bite," said Sunny, staring back at the one yellow eye.

"Muffler's been through a lot," Colin said, sounding as though he agreed. "I found him half dead and fixed him up, and he's been with me ever since."

Sunny gazed at the vision of Colin with the wreck of a cat in his arms. Colin was probably the first person who had ever loved him, fed him, petted him. In Colin's care a wild cat had become a huge, purring pussycat. With Colin, at least. He looked as though he'd like to throw her out of the house personally, and she wasn't sure he couldn't do it.

"Hello, Muffler," she said politely, rubbing the cat between the ears. Babe snarled. The purr intensified. Her ears itched from the vibration.

"He likes you," said Colin.

"However can you tell?"

"Because I know how he acts when he doesn't like somebody." He lowered Muffler to the table. "They'll be okay now," he said. "Want a house tour?"

"Sure," said Sunny, tightening her hold on Babe.

"Put him down," said Colin. "It'll be all right."

How do you know? Reluctantly she put Babe on the floor. Muffler jumped down to join him. Wishing she could give Babe a last goodbye, she left the two of them staring at each other, but when quiet prevailed, she was soon taking in Colin's house with a professional eye. From the kitchen, old-fashioned but efficient like hers, she wandered through a dining room with rich red walls and heavy, dark furniture into a prim parlor she suspected his mother had had a hand in decorating. Highly polished antiques gleamed at her from every nook and cranny. At last Colin led her into the library. "This is where I hang out," he said.

"It looks like you," Sunny said, feeling suddenly shy. The walls were lined with books, and she began reading the titles. He had everything, history and biography, books on architecture and art, science fiction and natural science, novels....

He came up behind her, circling her with his arms. She turned into his embrace, burying her head under his chin. All her worry about leading him on, about promising him too much, vanished in the urgency she always felt when he touched her. She tilted her face up to his.

His kiss was intense, fierce, reckless. In that kiss he revealed all the complexity of his feelings for her, and she spilled out her uncertainty in her quick, desperate response. His mouth devoured hers, his hands claimed her slim, bare arms, then met at the small of her back to pull her hard against him. His breath quickened as their bodies locked together in a parody of the ultimate caress, seeking and finding each other. She felt the slow ache of building desire, felt the dampness between her legs, felt his hard promise of relief.

"Let's take Babe home," she said breathlessly, "and go to our spot in the forest."

"Let's leave him here," said Colin. "Look at him."

While they kissed, Babe and Muffler had curled up together in the big wing chair, apparently planning a long nap. Muffler's huge paw was slung across Babe's back, and he was purring furiously. As she had feared he would, Babe had caught the country virus, had lost his aggressive fire and was now cuddling up to cats.

If she didn't keep her guard up, the same thing might happen to her.

10

SUNNY LAY BACK on the quilt and raised her arms to Colin. Pale light shafted through the trees, and a breeze cooled her skin. The quilt was soft, the bed of pine needles yielding. She moved against it, seeing desire quicken in his eyes.

He lowered his mouth to hers and settled there with a touch as light as a butterfly's. Her lips opened to him, inviting him to taste, to torment, to take this part of her, every part of her. She ran her hands down his arms, feeling the tautness of his muscles, knowing how brutally he reined himself in.

She made a soft sound of protest as he lifted his head to gaze at her. "You're irresistible, you know it?" he said. His smile was crooked, his voice husky.

"And yet you resist," she whispered back. "Be my love slave or I'll get out my spare leash."

"You don't need a leash. You've got me. I'm yours." His mouth came down to hers again, forceful and unyielding, but she gave herself fully to it, feeling the tenderness beneath, knowing he did no more than recognize and respond to her need. With one elbow to support the two of them, he effortlessly lifted her body to meet his fully. She pushed at him, pressed against him, seeking what she wanted from him.

SHE WANTED HIM, needed the tenderest loving care from him. He pulled her across himself, finding the freedom to caress every part of her. His hands slid down her undefended body, stopping to cup her breasts. Her nipples were tight and pointed, naked beneath her dress. The thought inflamed him. His fingers went to the zipper at the back and loosened it.

He knew this woman; he knew the clothes she liked to wear, the long soft cotton sundresses that hid the perfection of her body from the world, revealing only the slim delicacy of her arms and a tantalizingly small sample of her creamy, faintly freckled skin, yet gave the whole of her with such ease. Winter would come; those dresses would bloom into long-sleeved, high-necked ones, but she would still be there beneath, just as accessible, just as desirable. If winter came for the two of them.

Her body was so tempting that he couldn't waste time worrying about the future. She must know how urgently he desired her, and didn't she want him just as badly? Her hands, those deceptively delicate hands, moved into his hair, and he felt the small fingers tousling him, touching his ears, the base of his neck. In the grip of her caress, he knew nothing mattered, nothing but this magical moment.

NERVE ENDS UNCOILED from her scalp to the tips of her bare toes, then tensed with anticipation. She felt empty inside, incomplete, and tightened her arms around Colin as he sought her most private places, understanding the source of her most private longings. Her hand gripped his neck and she gasped as his tongue licked into her navel. He slid her dress down to the elastic of her panties, and his mouth traveled along the path to the wet and waiting part of her. He aroused her with a restraint that barely hid the intensity of his desire, yet it reduced the difference in their sizes to make her feel larger rather than smaller, a partner in his passion rather than a subject to it. She would make love with Colin and be sated, but she would also be soothed, warmed, comforted in the circle of his arms. She wanted that; she wanted it desperately.

But she also wanted him to be happy. She could bring him happiness now, in this way, but could she always?

What was this thing, "always"? It seemed very, very far away.

He was so swiftly inside her that she barely noticed the rustle of paper and foil. She gave herself up to him completely, knowing what passion he could bring up from the depths of her.

More than passion: He might be the man who could tear down the brick wall she'd built around her heart.

She couldn't take time just now to think about her heart. It was her body that begged for relief. Relief would be delicious, like a massive dam breaking and flooding a dry and barren plain. But she couldn't stop caring about him. If he broke down the brick wall, she didn't want him to get crushed in the rubble. She cared even now, when it was hard to think about anything but her own desires, to relish the way he took her, played her, moved with her, brought her to the highest peaks.

She fell over them, dizzy as she wafted downward, but at last at peace. And whatever her concerns about hurting him, they would have to wait. She had given him what he wanted while taking what she wanted. It was a gift from each of them to the other, unselfishly given, unselfishly received.

"WHERE HAVE WE BEEN?"

"You're not getting senile, are you, Colin? We've been—"

"You don't need to remind me," he said. "I've lost eleven pounds in the last hour. What I mean is, what do we tell the assembled witches when we go home?"

Sunny sat up, still naked, and crossed her legs in front

of her. Her face told him she intended to take the subject seriously. He, on the other hand, was hopelessly fascinated by the position she was sitting in.

"You assume they'll be lying in wait for us," she said.

"I know they'll be lying in wait for us."

"You assume they'll ask where we've been."

"I know they'll ask where we've been." *Focus on her face! No peeking!*

"Darn." Sunny seemed to be thinking hard. "We looked at your tile, we successfully introduced Muffler and Babe, and then we had dinner at a restaurant."

"What restaurant? Mother always wants to know."

"The Woodstock Inn."

"Where Uncle Amos and Aunt Eleanor have dinner almost every night?"

"Simon Pearce," Sunny said, "in Quechee."

"Where a grand-niece waits tables?" said Colin.

"We were on our way to Quechee..." said Sunny.

He could almost see her mind sharpen to a pencil point.

"...when we passed a motorist in trouble. Engine? Burned out. Emergency lights? Nonexistent, and night was inexorably falling. We couldn't leave him stranded there. We offered him a ride, and he said he was on his way to Roxbury, to the bedside of his dying mother...."

"Overused," said Colin, "and too depressing."

"...to the wedding of his beloved godchild..."

"Much better," he complimented her. "You're brilliant."

"I'm scared," said Sunny.

They gazed at each other. "Of what?" said Colin, stroking her cheek.

"A changing agenda," said Sunny. "Let's check each other for pine needles."

He didn't want to understand, but he did. Sunny had latched on to her only hope, to make a plan and stick to it.

Maybe all he had to do was introduce another plan to her. If she accepted it, then everything would be all right. If she didn't...

Colin couldn't think about "if she didn't" just now. "If she did" had energized him, renewed him, hardened the only part of him he could relate to at the moment.

"...AND THE POOR MAN was so upset," Sunny told Margaret. "What could we do but drive him to his godchild's wedding? Colin was a saint to do it," she added, helping herself to tiny helpings of warmed-up roast chicken, mashed potatoes and butternut squash for the third time. "I am so tired," she added, sinking back into her chair before attacking her plate. "He must be exhausted. He did all the driving."

"Not all," said Colin.

Sunny kicked him under the table.

"I'm just glad you're safely home," said Margaret Blalock. "Incidentally, Sunny, while I was looking for your end tables I found a baby dress in the attic, a little boy's christening dress from, oh, I'd guess the late eighteen hundreds. Would you like to have it?"

"Mother! For God's sake!" Colin hissed.

"For Babe," Margaret said, directing a look of utter innocence toward her son. "She might like to have him photographed in it. Rosamond, warm the biscuits for the raspberry shortcake, will you, while I make some fresh coffee. Martin, pour the children a little more wine to hold them until the coffee's ready."

ON A MORNING in late August, Colin saw the first orange leaves on Sunny's sugar maple tree. It was time for him to make a decision about her, time for her to make a decision about him. The cottage was almost finished.

"Break something," snapped Margaret Blalock.

"Flood the cellar," suggested Aunt Rosamond.

"A little wiring fire the next time Sunny goes to New York," said Martin Blalock, "would be the easiest thing to arrange. I'll do it myself if it bothers your conscience. I'd suggest the guest bathroom, where we wouldn't have to worry about furniture damage and it wouldn't inconvenience her too much...."

"Stop!" said Colin. "You've lost your minds, all of you."

"You've lost yours if you're going to stand by and watch Sunny put Woodbine Cottage on the market," Margaret said sternly.

"It wouldn't necessarily mean I'd lost Sunny," Colin argued. "Remember? You said so yourself, or started to. If we got married, we'd live in my house."

"You're getting married?" said his mother, looking weepy.

"Colin!"

"Son!"

"No," said Colin. "But..." He bit his lip. It wasn't the right time to tell them, but damn it, they were bugging him to death. "...I'm thinking about asking her."

A collective sigh of satisfaction rose like a wave around the kitchen table.

HER PIERCING SCREAM brought Margaret and Rosamond running to the cottage. "It's ruined," Sunny shrieked. "I'm ruined! What happened?"

In the scarlet silk suit she'd worn for doing business in New York, still clutching her small tapestry traveling bag, she stared wild-eyed at the wreck of her guest bathroom, the melted socket, the soot-stained tile, the singed wallpaper.

"There's been a fire in here," said Rosamond.

Well, of course there's been a fire in here. I didn't need anybody to tell me that! You think I'm an idiot? "I smelled it as soon as I walked in," Sunny wailed, squelching her more waspish reaction. "How could it have happened?"

"Lightning, I'd guess," said Margaret.

"Lightning," Rosamond agreed, nodding sagely, "does strange things."

"Lightning? Was there a storm while I was gone?"

"A violent electrical storm."

Of course the motherly Blalock women would struggle to remain calm about the disaster in hopes of soothing her. They didn't seem to be struggling, though. She eyed them contemplatively. "That's funny," she said. "I watched the weather reports while I was gone, and the New York stations didn't mention a thunderstorm."

"It came up unexpectedly," said Margaret.

"And left almost immediately," seconded Rosamond.

"No one but us would have been interested in it," said Margaret.

"I suppose not," said Sunny, accepting the answer. "I'd better call the insurance company."

"Don't bother," said Margaret.

"Colin will make it right," said Rosamond.

She heaved a sigh. "What timing. Just when the cottage was almost finished. And I found such a cute apartment on this trip."

"If it's right for you, it will be waiting for you when you're ready for it," Margaret assured her.

"That reminds me," said Sunny. "Which real estate agent do you recommend?" She whisked them out of the smoky bathroom and into the kitchen, where she reached into the refrigerator for a bag of coffee beans.

Margaret and Rosamond looked at each other. "I don't know," Margaret mused. "My cousin Helen used to be good, but she's gotten terribly absentminded."

"You will be, too, when you're eighty-four," said Rosamond. "There's Henry Carter, but he's so pushy."

Margaret snapped her fingers. "Evangeline Forrester," she said. "She moved to Bennington, but she does a lot of selling in the area. Very chic, Evangeline is."

"Oh, Margaret, do you think…"

"Yes, Rosamond," said Mrs. Blalock swiftly, turning to look directly at her sister-in-law, "Evangeline is precisely the right agent for Sunny to use."

Rosamond blinked. "Why, yes," she said. "I suppose she is."

"Okay, then," said Sunny, shouting over the whir of the coffee grinder. "Evangeline Forrester it is." At the sound of an engine she looked up, feeling the familiar heavy, hot sensation flood through her body. "It's Colin!" she said delightedly, and ran to meet him at the door.

LYING BACK LUXURIOUSLY against the blanket, Sunny stretched and yawned. "See," she said, "getting married isn't the only option."

"It's amazing, though," said Colin, who'd been looking for a way to introduce the topic, "how many weddings we have in September."

"Why September?"

"The first frost will turn this clearing into a whole new scene," said Colin. "When the leaves fall off the maples and poplars, you can see straight through to Mabel Forrester's chicken coop."

"You're kidding!" Sunny leapt up, rolling Colin off the blanket in her haste to wrap it around herself.

"We're on a hill in the middle of Latham Center," Colin said serenely, pulling on his underwear and jeans in one swift movement. "Below us to the right is the original Latham house, which fell into the hands of some in-laws back in the eighteen-eighties. Mrs. Forrester's off to the left.

You'd never know we were so close to civilization, would you?"

Sunny gripped the blanket in her teeth and pulled on her panties. "Drop my dress over my head, will you?" she asked him.

This one was flowered in violets with bright green leaves. Sunny's head appeared through the neckline, her eyes exactly the color of the leaves. Colin kissed her before she could pull the dress down over her knees.

"Happy?" he murmured.

"Very," she said. "I wish it never had to end."

Colin's heart pumped his heated blood faster. "Does it?"

"You said so," said Sunny. "Frost."

"You know what I mean," said Colin. He tilted her face up to his and confronted her directly, capturing her gaze as he would like to capture her. He was sorry, but not surprised, to find a look of fear in those huge green eyes. As he had guessed she would, she began to speak rapidly.

"Oh, I don't know, Colin," she said, turning her cheek to him. "I've had so many decisions to make in the last year I'm not sure I can handle another one. The separation and the divorce, and finding out I'd lost the apartment and gained a dog, and wondering what to do about the cottage, and…"

"I would never rush you, Sunny," Colin said, his lips brushing her cheek. "But if you go back to the city, I'm afraid we'll…" He tried to hold her, but she broke away.

"With all those decisions and all those worries, I had to make a plan for myself, and I'm afraid to start making changes in it." She slid slim feet into sandals the color of her sun-gilded legs. "I think I ought to go ahead with it, and then we'll see." She looked up quickly. "There's so much you don't know about me still, Colin. You don't even know my real name."

Suzann O'Brien wasn't her name? He had to admit this

was a shock. "Now might be a good time to tell me," he said, his mouth dry. She'd been misrepresenting herself? She'd been living under an alias? Why?

"Sunshine," she said almost inaudibly. "As in 'Let the Sunshine In.'"

Sunshine. Daughter of Starlight. Colin cupped his hands around her elbows so he could look into her face. "What's wrong with 'Sunshine'?" he said, relieved.

She turned away. "It reveals too much about Starlight and Poppa. They didn't spend a second wondering if the names people gave their children in those days, names like Sunshine and Love and Moonbaby, would stand the test of time. Not one of our founding fathers named a daughter Sunshine! You can't deny that."

He supposed he couldn't. "Well, now I know your name. What other skeletons do you have lurking in your closet?"

"That's it, mainly," said Sunny. "You already know the rest of my fatal flaws." She grabbed his hand, pulled the blanket up in a wad under her arm and led him toward the car. "Speaking of the cold weather, Babe's got to have some new coats. I stopped into Canine Creations when I was in New York, and they have the cutest little denim jacket lined in sheepskin. He could wear it when we come back to visit you, and they had a kilt, can you believe it? It was attached to a black wool coat with brass buttons. He'll wear that in the city. You've never seen anything so precious...."

Colin gritted his teeth. There were so many things about her he loved, but he had to keep reminding himself about her less lovable qualities—her obsession with city life, her rejection of her parents, and dammit, her insistence on dressing up her dog when there were children living on the hillsides a stone's throw from here who needed a winter coat a heck of a lot more than Babe did.

And yet he wanted her. His heart had stood still when

she said, "...when we come back to visit you." Did he want her enough to bear the cost of winning her? He had some painful thinking to do.

"ZIP ME UP?" said Sunny, turning away from him.

Colin gave himself a second to admire her slim little back before he took in the dress she was wearing. It was long, black and sleeveless. It had sequins all over it. He zipped it and turned her around. The green stem of a poppy climbed up the side of the dress, sent two leaves out across her stomach and exploded into a glittering red blossom across her bosom. It fit her so well it might have been pasted directly on her body. He wanted to run his hands down the length of it, but the risk of slashing them on sequins was too great.

"Isn't it a little formal for a Labor Day cookout in my folks' back yard?"

"Oh, you," Sunny said affectionately. "This is what I'm wearing to the Amons' fiftieth wedding anniversary party in a couple of weeks. I was trying it on to be sure I can still fit into it, and I must say it's a stretch. Your mother's cooking is ruining my figure. I'm wearing shorts to the cookout. Okay, you can unzip me now."

"This is the part I like," Colin murmured, slowly unzipping the dress, then running his hands across the bare, creamy skin beneath.

She shivered deliciously. "Cut it out," she said sternly. "Your mother sets the kitchen timer for five minutes every time you walk into this house, and if you haven't come out when it goes off she calls your aunt Rosamond."

"Five minutes is enough," said Colin indistinctly, his mouth buried in her hair.

She giggled. "Not for me." She slipped out of his embrace. Happily, she next slipped out of the dress. Unhappily, it took her a flat ninety seconds to skim into silky white bikini panties, white shorts that were just the right length to turn him on beyond endurance while not offending his family, a bra, of all things, and a polo shirt the color of her eyes. Where was the long, yielding sundress he'd gotten used to?

"Babe," she called, "come out, come out, wherever you are. Time to go."

Colin looked down to see Babe slinking through the door dressed in what appeared to be an archaic military uniform. "Sunny," he said slowly, "just this once couldn't you let him go without an outfit on?" He saw the quick hurt fill her eyes and he was sorry, but this was important to him.

"Not wear his Green Mountain Boys uniform to the party?"

"Not wear anything to the party."

Hurt gave way to anger. "Why not? He doesn't mind."

"How do you know he doesn't mind? Don't you think those clothes hold him back? Why don't you spend the money outfitting a deprived kid or two?"

"I can do both," she snapped. "Come on, Colin, lighten up."

They stared at each other for a tense moment, then Colin shrugged. "At least let him take off the uniform to play in the wading pool with the kids."

"Oh, sure," said Sunny, but her eyes looked a trifle shifty to him. "He's got a swimsuit for playing in the pool. Shall we go?"

11

"WHAT A GREAT PARTY," said Sunny as Colin walked her home. "Don't be a tease," she added, as he whirled her toward him in the kitchen. "Remember your mother's kitchen timer."

Colin sighed. "What did you and Belinda talk about for such a long time?"

Sunny hesitated while she pulled off Babe's wet swim-suit—a twenties-style one-piece in red and white stripes—and spread it over a chair to dry. Babe drank long and thirstily from his water bowl, then trotted away, presumably in search of a good night's sleep. "Clothes," she said at last.

"Dumb question," he groused.

She'd decided not to tell him she had made a large contribution to a volunteer organization Belinda had founded, one which provided clothing for needy children. She'd sworn Belinda to secrecy, too. There was something else she wanted to discuss with him. Something important. "Colin…" she began.

"Mmm?"

She began to walk back toward her bedroom and he followed. Babe lay in his bed, out cold from his active afternoon. She kicked off her sandals, swiped a pale pink lip gloss across her sun-dried mouth and whisked a brush through her tangled hair. "Will you go with me to the Amons' anniversary party?" In the dressing-table mirror she caught his expression, surprised, uncertain, then uneasy.

"I don't think I…"

"Don't say no without considering it," she protested. "I have to go down to the city early next week to put their apartment together. You could take the train on Thursday or even Friday, just so you'll have enough time to rent a tuxedo…"

"Tuxedo."

"Well, yes. It's a black-tie affair. You'll look gorgeous in a tuxedo."

His eyes were rebellious. "I don't ever want to put on a tuxedo again."

"What do you mean 'again'?" she asked, her hairbrush poised. "You put on a tuxedo for some other woman and you won't put one on for me?"

"That was a long time ago," Colin said slowly.

"And you must tell me about it sometime. But that's not the point," Sunny hurried on. "The point is I'm only asking you to do it once. It couldn't be that painful, just one night in a tuxedo. Babe's wearing one, and he…"

The minute the words were out of her mouth she knew she couldn't have said anything worse, or at a worse time, if she'd scripted it.

"Babe? Has a tuxedo?" His face reddened, his eyebrows drew together, his eyes darkened to the color of slate, his mouth drew a line as thin as shale. He straightened, his shoulders stiffened and his fingertips curled. He was on his way to forming fists. The fact that he was mad would have been hard to miss.

"He does now," she said, determinedly cheerful. "I bought it big, so he'll only have to have one. I'll show it to you. You can see how adorable it is, and you can just imagine how cute he's going to look in it…"

Colin merely stared as she brought the box from Canine Creations down from a shelf in her closet and spread out the little costume on the bed. His expression was so forbidding, and the silence so electric, that for the first time in many years Sunny didn't choose to leap into it feet first. Her feet, she was sure, would go straight for her mouth.

Following his gaze, examining the tuxedo herself, she began to feel sort of silly. It was not until today, talking with Belinda, that she'd realized that dressing her dog might not be the best use of her money. But Babe Ruth was her baby...

Maybe what she really wanted was a baby to hold and cuddle and comfort and, yes, buy clothes for... She took a deep, quivery breath. The man she'd like to have that baby with was looking at her as though she was a freak.

"Very cute," said Colin, "and so are you, but Sunny..." He spread out his arms in mute appeal. "Don't you care about anything important, anything at all?"

"Of course I do," she retorted. "I care about Babe, I care about..."

"No, you don't. He's just a toy to you, a doll to play with until you get bored. You feel the same way about the cottage. I expect you feel the same way about me."

"That's not true! I care very deeply about..."

"Sure," said Colin, "like you care about your parents. That should have tipped me off, but I was falling in love and stupid enough to think you'd change."

"Falling in love?" Sunny said, her voice faltering. "You were..."

"You think I would have made love to you if I hadn't been?"

The very air in the room hummed with tension. "No," Sunny whispered. "And neither would I."

It shook him. She could see him begin to realize what she'd just said, could see uncertainty begin to make inroads into his anger. For a moment she felt hopeful that this scene would soon end, that they'd forget it ever happened, but his words destroyed that hope.

"I'm not sure you know what love is," he said.

The pain growing inside her became too sharp to deal with. The defenses she'd learned through the years rose in a wall of anger. "You got that right," she said breezily. "I probably don't." She breathed a stagy sigh, trying to control the tremor in her voice. "So I'm probably not the woman for you."

Colin clenched his teeth. When he spoke, his voice rasped. "Let me tell you about the woman I wore a tuxedo for."

"I shall hang on every word." He clearly didn't appreciate her flippant attitude, but she would never let him know the anxiety it masked.

"Her name was Lisa. I thought I loved her. I thought she loved me. She said she loved my family..."

"And they took her to their bosom?" A long time ago or not, she was jealous.

She didn't know how his jaw could tighten any further, but it did. "They would have eventually," he said. "But they didn't have a chance. As soon as I asked her to marry me, she began trying to turn me into the person she wanted me to be, an architect in Boston, dressed up in a suit by day and a tuxedo by night. Sure, she loved Vermont, loved my family—as long as they kept their distance. Fortunately I found out in time. I tried it her way and found out I wanted to be here. I still want to be here, Sunny. This is where I belong. I want a wife who's happy here, too. I want to bring up my children here..."

"Not with me," she said. She'd meant it as a question, had hoped he would protest. Maybe she should have made it sound like a question. Tears were stinging her eyes. She had to get this over with before he noticed.

He paled. His body froze in place, but when he finally spoke, his voice had lightened. He sounded calm, matter-of-fact, merely a bit rueful. "Maybe not," he said. "Maybe you shouldn't have children. Maybe your only interest in children is dressing them up.''

His words hung in the heated air. She fought back the tears, tilted her chin and gave him a stubborn smile. "I might be capable of a little more than that,'' she said. "Look at the social graces I've taught Babe.''

Colin gazed at her. "Look,'' he said finally, "we're both tired and tense for one reason or another. I don't know how this conversation ended up the way it did. Why don't we take some time to calm down, talk it over reasonably—after you get back from the Amons' party. I'm not going with you, Sunny.'' He gave her a crooked smile. "I might wear a tuxedo for you someday so you can see how *cute* I look, but not this time.''

Sunny lifted Babe out of his bed and cuddled him next to her while she cried herself to sleep. She was afraid that when she and Colin "talked it over,'' it would be their last conversation.

There was only one way to get rid of the tight, anxious knot in the pit of her stomach. She had to get out of Vermont forever. The next morning, she called Evangeline Forrester.

SHE DISLIKED Evangeline at first sight. Since she usually liked people at first sight, she spent a minute analyzing her reaction. Evangeline was in her mid-forties, tall, blond, assured and really quite pretty in her flowing blue silk shirtwaist, but her voice had that affected whine that made Sunny think her name should be Muffy. Or Twinkie. And when Babe welcomed her by jumping up on her, Evangeline skated away from him as though he were a rat, murmuring nervously about her stockings.

"It's such a *sweet* house,'' Evangeline whinnied as Sunny showed her through. "How far away is the skiing?''

That was another thing: Evangeline saw Woodbine Cot-

tage entirely in terms of selling points. She looked out the
kitchen windows onto Sunny's flourishing garden and little
flagstone patio set in the middle of lush bluegrass. "Plenty
of room to expand," Evangeline said. "That's a good selling point."

"Expand into my herbs and flowers?" said Sunny.
"Tear up my patio?"

"But, dear…" Evangeline fixed her with a wide, bright
smile. "It won't be yours anymore. You'll never know."

"Of course not," said Sunny. "How silly of me."

"Yes," said Evangeline, making notes on a pink pad
with a sharp pencil. She put the pencil away, got out a pen.
"So if you'll sign right here…" She frowned. "This price
is awfully high," she commented.

"Woodbine Cottage is special," Sunny insisted. "Its historic value is priceless."

"I'll do my best," said Evangeline. She pressed the pen
into Sunny's hand.

"Maybe I shouldn't sign anything until—" *until I tell
Colin* "—until the bathroom wallpaper is up."

"A small detail," Evangeline said smoothly. "I promised you I wouldn't show it to a *soul* until you're back
from your little do in New York."

Sunny's hand shook a little as she signed "Suzann
O'Brien" to an agreement to list Woodbine Cottage with
one Evangeline Forrester of Forrester Realty for a period
of ninety days. "Ugh!" she burst out as soon as the woman
was out of the house. "If the Blalock women hadn't rec-
ommended her," she declared to Babe, "I would never
have put this lovely house in her…"

A loud thwacking sound, rhythmic and repeated, interrupted Sunny's moment of regret. She went to the parlor
window to see Evangeline driving a For Sale sign into the
ground. Surely it was too soon to put up a sign!

She was dashing out to tell Evangeline to take her sign

and go home when Evangeline backed out of her driveway and Colin's truck pulled in to the Blalocks'. She saw his eyes focus on the sign, saw the muscles chisel his face. He stopped the truck, got out, approached the sign, read it. It all seemed to happen in slow motion. He reached out, grasped the post the sign was nailed to and wrenched it out of the ground.

Then the action speeded up. Colin charged toward her door, wielding the sign like a shield. "What is this?" he demanded to know.

"A For Sale sign," Sunny said in a very small voice.

"What's it doing in your yard?"

"Telling people the cottage is for sale?" said Sunny.

"You couldn't even tell me about it first?"

"I was going to tell you the next time I saw you," Sunny said. "I didn't know Evangeline was going to dart right out and hammer a sign into the ground."

"I thought we were going to talk about it when you got back from New York."

"I already heard what you were going to say—last night," Sunny said.

Colin stared at her, his blue eyes stormy. "Is this what you want?"

"It's what I have to do." She gazed back evenly.

Colin slowly lowered the sign to the ground. Faceup or facedown, it still said For Sale. "I'll send Mike over to paper the bathroom as soon as I can get him off the Samuelsons' project," he said. His voice was low and controlled.

"Samuelsons!" said Sunny, distracted. "Who are they? What happened to the Larribees? Don't I come before the Samuelsons?"

A little of his control slipped. "Not officially," he snapped. "You bullied your way into the Larribees' time, and that spilled over into the Samuelsons' time. Time runs out here, Sunny, when the ground freezes!''

"My time's running out, too!" Not wanting the conversation to degenerate into the kind of fight they'd had last night, she made herself calm down. "There are two times to sell, spring and fall. And it's fall." She glanced at the maple tree that shaded her yard and driveway. Every day there were a few more orange leaves.

"Yes," he murmured, "it is." Whatever the thought that ran through his mind, it had diminished his anger. "I guess you have to—get ready for winter."

"I'm glad you're able to look at it that way," said Sunny.

"I have to do the same thing," Colin said. "Do what's best for me, in other words, no matter how it affects...others."

Sunny didn't like his tone. Of course he was right; if she could forge ahead with selling the cottage no matter how it affected him, then he could forge ahead with—what? She could think of any number of things he might want to forge ahead with that she wouldn't want him to at all! But she'd gotten herself in a corner. "Yes," she said bravely. "You must."

"Okay, then," he said, "I will."

With long strides, he covered the distance to his parents' kitchen door, threw it open to let himself in and slammed it with an original-windowpane-shattering crash. Sunny winced. Colin of all people ought to know better.

ANGRY OR NOT, Colin finished the cottage. At least, his crew did; Colin was conspicuously absent. "Finding more crew," he said coolly on one occasion when she caught a glimpse of him.

The anxious knot in her stomach only grew during her trip to New York to install the Amons' decor and attend their anniversary party. The apartment fell into place like the pieces of a child's jigsaw puzzle. When she placed the cleaned, restored celery green pouf in the center of their formal drawing room, she burst into tears and was forced to tell Van about her disastrous summer fling.

She had barely recovered when the Amons arrived to view with delight the recreation of their honeymoon apartment, but Colin was still on her mind. "Why did you choose September for your wedding?" she asked Mrs. Amon, who had come from an era of June brides.

"We wanted to get married before the ground froze," Mrs. Amon said cryptically.

"Adelaide!" said Howard Amon, scandalized.

Sunny blushed; Van and Adelaide tittered.

Even zipping up the poppy dress on Saturday evening reminded her of Colin. Ready at last, she looked at Babe. "Time to get into your tux," she said enthusiastically, hoping to psych him up for the evening. "Jump jump. Up on the bed so I can reach you better."

Babe looked at her suspiciously and didn't move. "Come on, sweetie, we're already late." He looked away. It was his "Who, me?" pose.

"You cairn terriers are so stubborn." She gave him an affectionate smile. "Okay, young man, do you want to go to the party?" At the magic word *go*, Babe began dancing around the room. "Then you'll have to…"

She paused. Colin wended his way into her thoughts, Colin pushing his nephew Scooter on the swing, Colin cuddling his shabby, battered cat, Muffler, Colin telling her, "Maybe you shouldn't have children."

She felt the ache of tears behind her eyelids and tilted her head back so they wouldn't spoil her makeup. When the tears passed, she found Babe gazing at her, his head cocked to one side. "You don't have to wear the tux if you don't want to," she said softly.

WHEN SHE STEPPED into the cottage at the end of the long drive from New York, she was surprised by the feeling that she was coming home. The answering-machine light blinked at her. With a rush of hope that Colin might have called, she played back the messages.

The cool voice that emerged from the machine startled her so badly that she dropped her cup of tea on the kitchen floor. While the saucer rolled crazily across the boards, Dexter's voice said: "Sunny. I hear you're going to be in New York this week. Bring Babe Ruth by while you're here, okay? Save us all a lot of hassle. Don't bother with his stuff. Marielle's got him a bunch of new things. Give me a call, set up a time."

The next message was also from Dexter, but this time Sunny listened more stoically. "Sunny. Maybe my earlier call didn't catch you before you left Vermont, but I know you'll be checking your messages. Marielle and I are home all weekend. Bring Babe by any time after, oh, noonish."

"I'm not going to call him," she told Babe, who hadn't reacted at all to the sound of his master's voice. "He has some crazy idea he's got custody and I don't even want to talk to him about it."

"Sunny!" said Dexter in his third message, "I insist on clearing up the matter of Babe Ruth. Call me at once. I hope I don't have to drive up there and get him!"

"He's just bluffing," Sunny reassured Babe. There was a fourth message.

"I'll be bringing the Anstadts by tomorrow at four o'clock sharp," Evangeline neighed. "Could you make yourself scarce? And take the dog with you?"

But there was no word from Colin.

THE NEXT AFTERNOON Sunny wandered disconsolately into her back yard, imagining a three-story addition surging up from the earth where her lupines were just getting settled in. She was startled when Rosamond called to her over the fence. The look on the woman's face was somewhere between sympathetic and funereal. The family knew things were not going well between Colin and her.

"Come in and have a bite of sesame tea cake," Rosamond enticed her.

"Well…" Sunny debated with herself. "You would actually be doing me a great favor to let us visit a while. Someone's coming to look at the cottage. I should get in the car and leave, but…"

"But you want to see what the people look like."

"Exactly," said Sunny.

Rosamond giggled like a schoolgirl. "We'll spy out the windows."

Sunny shouldn't have been surprised to see Margaret sitting at Rosamond's kitchen table cutting into a square frosted cake dotted with toasted sesame seeds, but she was. "Hello, Mrs. Blalock," she said. She nibbled at her lower lip, then decided to get everything out in the open. "I'm afraid your son is very angry at me."

"We can still be friends," Colin's mother said placidly. "Call me Margaret."

"Margaret's right," said Rosamond. "Time we were on a first-name basis."

This symbol of acceptance into West Latham undid Sunny completely. *Don't make a fool of yourself,* she thought fiercely, struggling to control a sudden, surprising wash of tears, but it didn't work. The tears flowed.

"It seems like the worst possible time to me," she wailed. "I'm so sorry I have to sell the cottage. You've been so kind to me, just like a moth…moth…" She couldn't go on.

It took a minute more to get the tears under control, particularly with Margaret's arm around her shoulders and her quiet, "There, there, shh…"

"Rosamond, I have so much to thank you for, too," said Sunny, "your tools and your cuttings and all your advice…"

"It's not as though we were saying goodbye," said Rosamond. Something in her tone, in the glance she exchanged with Margaret, made Sunny suspect that the Blalock women hadn't given up on this match.

"Have a piece of Rosamond's cake?" said Margaret. "It's quite good."

"Thank you," said Sunny, and took a bite. It was more than quite good. She sighed deeply, feeling better already.

"I wouldn't say Colin is angry," said Margaret as though there had not been a break in the conversation. "I'd say he's upset."

"So am I," said Sunny, "but I guess we just aren't right for each other." It took all her willpower and another bite of cake to sound so matter-of-fact.

"We all thought you seemed terribly right for each other," said Margaret.

Sunny sighed again. "Colin's life is here, where his work is," she said, "and mine is in the city, where my work is. I have to support myself."

Their faces told her she didn't have to support herself entirely, not with Colin to help out. It was a pleasant daydream, to go on working without feeling desperate to make a lot of money, to feel she had someone to fall back on. She shook herself. It was just that, a daydream. You couldn't fall back on anyone but yourself, your savings, your careful planning for an uncertain future.

"How do you like Evangeline?" said Rosamond.

The change in topic was so sudden it startled Sunny. "She's, ah, she's certainly a go-getter," said Sunny. "I told her she couldn't show the house until I got back from New York. That was yesterday, and here she is with the first prospects."

The three women rushed as a single feminine force to the window. Sunny saw an elegant couple emerge from Evangeline's luxurious car, saw them pause, and saw them gaze at the cottage reflectively.

Mrs. Anstadt immediately pointed at something near the roofline. Mr. Anstadt followed the trajectory described by her finger and nodded gravely. Evangeline's face registered protest.

Sunny's eyes narrowed. "They're already criticizing something," she said. "Probably that spot where the paint is starting to peel."

"Look how thin her lips are," said Rosamond.

"Mean," Margaret agreed.

"Eaters of salad exclusively," said Sunny. "And the odd razor blade." They fell silent, waiting. The Anstadts had gone into the house, and she wanted to see their expressions when they came out. When she was close to exploding with tension, they appeared. "Did you see that face she made?" Sunny asked.

"Their offer will probably be contingent on dozens of things they want you to do to the cottage," said Margaret comfortably.

"What things?" said Sunny. "It's perfect! Besides, nobody who made a face like that would make an offer. And they didn't stay long. Speaking of which, I've overstayed my welcome. Thanks," she said, trying to compress everything she felt into her smile. "Come on, Babe, let's go home."

Since no one seemed inclined to give him another bite of cake, Babe was willing.

12

"BECAUSE IT'S NOT SQUARE!" Colin yelled. "Look at it. Any fool could see it isn't... I'm sorry," he said immediately. "I didn't mean that, and you know it." He gave Mike, his finest framer, occasional wallpaperer and lifetime friend, a dour half smile.

"You're not yourself today," Mike said. "Girl trouble?"

"No girl," said Colin.

"That's what I call trouble," said Mike.

"Can we get on with the job?" said Colin, tight-lipped.

"Yes, master," said Mike.

Colin muttered an expletive and stalked off to see what else was going wrong at the Samuelsons' project. He couldn't find anything, which only made him madder. Nothing would make him feel good right now except taking that For Sale sign down from Woodbine Cottage and crushing it into a million splinters with his bare hands.

Instead he went home. He lay down on the sofa in the study and stared at the ceiling. There was a crack in it! His whole life was falling down on his head! And crushing his chest! "Hey, Muffler, take it easy," he wheezed. Muffler purred.

If only she had loved the cottage, she could have loved him. Why did he have to fall in love with another Lisa? Damn, he was exhausted, he was lonely and his libido was giving him fits. It seemed like an eternity since he last made love to Sunny and his need was insistent, blotting out important thoughts he should be having, like how to organize the next steps of the Samuelson project, how to finish up the plumbing before the plumber stole anything, how to get Ted's mind off the novel he and his wife were working on. He bet contractors in New York didn't have problems that crazy.

It would feel good to dump all this on his parents, but he didn't want to run into Sunny. He was especially eager not to run into Sunny until he'd pulled off his little surprise. He wondered what Kate's family was up to tonight. Before he could call her, the telephone rang.

"Sunny got an offer for Woodbine Cottage from the first couple who looked at it," his mother said without preamble.

He felt almost sick at his stomach. "She must be happy," he said tonelessly.

"She turned it down."

"Why?" said Colin. "The offer was low?"

"She didn't like the people," said his mother. "Well, goodbye, dear. I just wanted to keep you informed."

Hearing the dial tone, Colin slammed down the receiver. Another miserable, aching night passed.

"THE SMYTHES want to make an offer to you personally," said Evangeline. "I'll bring them over this afternoon."

With time to kill, Sunny went out into the garden to pinch dead blooms off the petunias and divide hostas for planting beneath the maple tree. She was still gardening when a brace of long, expensive cars, Evangeline's and the Smythes', pulled up to the cottage.

"May we go inside?" Jacqueline Smythe asked. "Before we make an offer, Bert and I want to ask you a few questions about the neighborhood." Dressed in cashmere and silk from gold necklace to Italian shoe, she looked Sunny up and down as though she were gauging the credibility of a person whose jeans knees were filthy and whose oversize sweatshirt, a consolation gift from Bev, said Throw pots. Not grenades.

"Of course," Sunny said, trying for a warm, welcoming smile and sensing she'd achieved more of a snarl. "I'll make coffee."

"We wondered," said Mrs. Smythe when she'd settled herself on the faded chintz sofa in the parlor, "what your neighbors were like."

"They're Lathams and Blalocks," she said, already offended by Mrs. Smythe's attitude. "Their ancestors founded this town."

"What Jacqueline means," said Bert Smythe, "is that we've met a few longtime Vermonters we wouldn't care to live next door to." His jowls quivered.

"We'll only be here for ski weekends with the children," explained Jacqueline. "We'll install a security system, of course, but we still don't want to leave the place unattended if the neighbors are the sort who might—"

"The Blalocks are wonderful people," Sunny said. A pulse throbbed at her temple and her face flushed with anger. "Margaret Blalock and her sister-in-law Rosamond have become my close friends. I can assure you—"

"But are they quiet?" Bert said. "It's important that my weekends be restful."

"Well—" A snappish, "Well of course they're quiet," was on the tip of her tongue, but she bit it back. She gazed through the arched parlor doorway across to the open window in the guest room. Framed by the white tieback curtains, Rosamond searched for butternuts among the brilliant leaves. She carried a beautiful old egg basket, and in her tweed trousers and soft green sweater set she was a vision of regal elegance. She was just the sort of person the Smythes would like to live next door to, someone to caricature boastfully to their friends in Boston.

"Excuse me," she said politely. "The coffee must be ready."

"Psst," she hissed out the kitchen door, then darted into the yard and gestured for Rosamond to come closer. "Go inside and play the organ," she said.

Rosamond looked put off. "Am I bothering the prospective buyers out here in my own yard?"

"Not nearly enough. Play 'Lady of Spain,' and pull out all the stops!"

Rosamond's eyes opened wide. "But Sunny, I'm still learning 'Lady—'"

"That's the whole idea."

Rosamond grasped her meaning instantly. "I'll give it my all," she said.

Sunny quickly assembled the coffee tray and returned to the parlor. "As I was about to say," she began, "my neighbors are lovely people, very quiet, churchgoers and upstanding citizens. You'll never know they're there. Why, sometimes I feel as though I'm all alone out in the country, with no one but me within miles—"

With a wheezing start, the thunderous chords of "Lady of Spain" blasted through the open windows from Rosamond's house, accompanied by a tremulous, off-key, "La-dy of Spay, nia-dore you, all of my lie, fie live for youuuuu, La-dy—"

"Rosamond Blalock is quite musical," said Sunny, speaking loudly. She noticed with great pleasure that Evangeline had paled, and her pencil was twitching. "She missed being church organist by a hair. Emily Carter used political pressure, we're sure, to get the job. Rosamond practices constantly, though. She wants to be ready if the congregation ever puts it to a vote again."

She had to raise her voice another notch, because from Margaret Blalock's open sitting-room windows just a stone's throw from Sunny's parlor, the familiar opening theme of "All My Children" almost blew Sunny off the footstool where she had perched to serve coffee. It seemed that Rosamond had taken time to pass the word on to Margaret. Sunny held up a protesting hand. "You won't have to worry about Margaret and her penchant for the soaps," she said reassuringly. "They don't air on weekends, and her husband's not as deaf."

"Not as deaf?" Jacqueline said faintly.

"As she is. Football is his thing," Sunny explained. "College games all day Saturday, pro ball on Sunday. But you'll hear almost nothing except the band playing, unless he gets mad at the coach, or his team wins. Or loses."

"Jacqueline—" said Bert.

"Bert—" said Jacqueline. They exchanged loaded glances. "We'll think about it," said Jacqueline. "We'd better be going, Evangeline."

"You did that on purpose!" Evangeline quavered when the Smythes were out of earshot.

"I didn't like them," Sunny said.

"You'll never sell this house if you keep driving people away!" shrilled Evangeline, watching her last prospects drive away.

"Of course I will," Sunny said. "I could have sold it two times already. There will be a third. I simply will not sell Woodbine Cottage to people who won't love it as I do, and care for it as I have—"

"Sunny!" Evangeline yelled, leaving her nasal passages out of her delivery. "It's a *house!* You're *selling* it! You're not giving it up for adoption!"

Her blue jersey wrap dress swirled around her calves as she spun toward the front door. She paused. She peered through the window toward Sunny's drive. "My goodness," she said, diverted. "Who in the world is that with Colin?"

The sound of his name, even when it was spoken by

Evangeline, sent Sunny rushing across the hall to join her. Colin's Corvette was parked in Sunny's drive, and a man and a woman were emerging from it. "Domestic help, you suppose, or a new crew member?" said Evangeline.

"Crew member!" Sunny screamed. "That's Poppa!"

"SURPRISED, SUNSHINE?" Sunny's father, a slim redhead, gave her a bear hug.

"Oh, my, yes," Sunny said dully. "Hi, Starlight. Good trip?"

"Colin here said you would be," Laurence O'Brien said. "Surprised."

"A lovely trip," Starlight said dreamily. "Colin bought our tickets, picked us up at the airport... I felt like royalty."

They stood awkwardly in the center hall of the cottage. Sunny gazed at her mother, thinking how pretty she looked with her graying blond hair pulled back in a ponytail, a long, fanciful skirt brushing the tops of her sandals. Her eyes, green like Sunny's, were sparkling with excitement at this new adventure.

And then she looked at Colin. If she'd ever seen a more smug, more self-satisfied, more evilly victorious expression on a human face she couldn't remember when. "How very kind of him," she said, glaring at the object of her sudden rage.

"He invited us to stay with him, too," said Starlight, "until we can afford a place of our own."

"Nonsense," Sunny snapped. "You'll stay with me."

"No, no," said Colin. "We don't want to put you out. With the house for sale, it'll be easier on everybody if—"

"They—will—stay—with—me!" Sunny said through clenched teeth. "They're my parents, for heaven's sake. They will stay in my house! Bring in your stuff," she directed the O'Briens.

"I'll get it," said Colin.

"You will stay right here and have a little chat with me," said Sunny, sounding rather like royalty herself. "Why did you do it?" she ranted as soon as Starlight and Laurence were out the front door. "You knew, I told you, that—"

"You told me we all have to do what's best for ourselves in the long run," Colin said piously, pressing his hands to his heart. "I needed a crew member, I found one."

"How?" Sunny said desperately.

"I have ways," said Colin.

"Bev!" Sunny snarled.

"She was one way," Colin admitted.

Sunny was beyond rage, beyond speech. "Well," she spluttered, "well—"

"Where shall we put our things, honey?" said Starlight, opening the front door.

"In here," said Sunny, gesturing toward the guest room door. Silently she watched cardboard suitcases, toolboxes, a guitar case and several plastic bags flood through the door. A bread pan stuck out of the top of one of the bags. A large carton was labeled Spinning Wheel.

Laurence O'Brien looked at Sunny, then at Colin. "Star and I will do a little unpacking," he said.

"Fine," said Sunny, glaring silently at Colin, while her father closed the door. "You put words in my mouth," she accused him. "You said I was 'doing what was best for me, regardless of its effects on others,' and that gave *you*..."

"...must introduce us to your parents," said Margaret Blalock, popping her head through the front door. Rosamond's head appeared beside hers. "Just a quick hello, then we'll be on our way. Do bring your family to dinner tonight, won't you? I know this was a surprise. You can't be prepared to cook a big meal. I'm doing a prime rib roast."

"Ah-h-h..." Sunny stammered. The phone rang. It was Evangeline Forrester. "Sure," Sunny said grimly, "bring them over at seven. Yes, Evangeline, the coast will be clear. We'll all be next door at the Blalocks'." If she could possibly wipe Colin off the face of the earth with a prime rib, she was certainly going to give it a try.

"IT'S THE HOME we've been saving for," said Elizabeth Blalock Carter. Her blue eyes shone. She buried her face in her baby son's dark curls and hugged him tight.

"It doesn't need anything," said Richard Latham Carter. He sounded awed. "We can move right in."

"If I'd decorated the house myself," said Elizabeth, "I would have done it just this way."

"The price…" said Sunny.

"…is fine," Richard said firmly. "Evangeline's on her way over with the earnest money contract."

"The terms…"

"Cash. The bank has already approved our mortgage."

"You want to move in…"

"…at your convenience."

"Your families will be popping in and out all the time," Sunny said, her eyes narrowing. "Won't that be a bother?"

"It's why we came back," said Elizabeth. "We've been working and saving for ten years so Richard could set up a law practice right here at home. We want Latham to grow up here, where we did, *like* we did, surrounded by family."

"I need to think about it," Sunny said when Evangeline presented her with the contract.

"Think about what?" screeched Evangeline.

"Things," said Sunny.

"Of course you need to think about it," said Elizabeth. "I can imagine how painful it would be to leave this place."

"Take your time," said Richard. "Mother's happy to have us as long as we need to stay."

Damn it, were these people perfect? Sunny glowered at their parting smiles.

LAURENCE O'BRIEN fit into his crew like the missing cog. Colin put him right onto the finish work at the Larribees' house, and was amazed at the progress the crew was suddenly making. He decided it was time to come out of his slump and make a little progress himself.

"Ceramic tile is *yesterday*. French limestone is in," tonight's date said. "Colin, that cat is making me extremely nervous. Why is he staring at me that way?"

"Mmm," said Colin, stifling a yawn. "He just does that. Have a seat, make yourself comfortable. Gin and tonic, right?" He started for the kitchen.

He'd gritted his teeth and asked Irene the tile supplier out. Drinks at home, dinner at a restaurant in Ludlow. He was sorry he'd asked her out the minute he arrived at her house to pick her up. He'd forgotten how hefty she was, and how practical. He was tired of talking tile, and it was only six-thirty. The night loomed long in front of him. There wasn't the slightest chance he would choose to spend it with her.

Her shriek made a dent in his boredom. Colin dashed back to the library. "He scratched me!" said Irene. She held out her arm. Long red marks confirmed her diagnosis. A few drops of blood oozed from the broken skin. "Omigod," Colin muttered. "Muffler! Scat! Hang on, Irene. I'll get some witch hazel."

He'd bunched up the witch hazel and bandages under his arm when the phone rang. "What!" he growled into the receiver.

"That's how you speak to your mother?" said Margaret Blalock. "I just wanted to tell you Sunny has an offer from

Cousin Richard and his wife Elizabeth. They're the dearest couple, and have the cutest baby..."

He heard a scream from the library. "We'll have to talk about it later, Mother." His voice shook. "I've got a situation here."

"YOU AND POPPA go see the house by yourselves," Sunny said.

She glanced around the cottage. Starlight had unpacked her bread pans, her guitar, her spinning wheel. The cottage smelled of rising bread, rich vegetable stews, cinnamon and damp fleece. She couldn't find a single excuse for rejecting the Carters' offer, but before she accepted it, she had to relocate her parents. Evangeline had found a house in South Latham that sounded just right for them. The newspaper ad she faxed over read "Lots of charm, needs TLC."

"If you're sure you won't go with us…" Starlight said. She wore a white peasant blouse with a long calico skirt. She'd pulled her hair back with a bow, and in Sunny's eyes, she was absolutely beautiful. She'd always thought her mother was beautiful, especially when they sat together on the grass while Starlight played the guitar and Sunny sang along. All these years, had she only remembered the bad times? Poppa's red hair was graying, too. They weren't old, but one day they would be, and she wouldn't be too far away to look after them.

Her stomach clenched again. She wanted to be here to look after them.

What? No! I want to be in New York!

Think again. I want to be here. I want to be here with Colin. I want to have a family just like Elizabeth and Richard Carter's.

She felt stunned. How could she just now be admitting

to herself what she really wanted? How could she have thought her life would ever be complete without Colin?

How could she have imagined she would give him up without a fight?

"You're the ones who will have to live in the house," she said shakily, groping her way back to the present. "Now, Poppa," she warned him, "you know what 'needs TLC' means. It needs tender, loving care. That means it's a mess. It needs work."

"My kind of work," her father said, rubbing his hands together.

"Then take the Jeep and get going," Sunny urged them. She needed time to think, to plan, to restructure her life. "It looks like we're going to have a storm."

She and Babe went into the front yard to wave them off. The sky did indeed look threatening, and the air was still and heavy, unusual for Vermont in early fall. "Come on, Babe, let's put those clothes out for Belinda to pick up," she said.

In the last few days she had decided she had far too many clothes. She'd made a merciless raid on her closets and the still-packed wardrobe boxes. Her fake-fur coats and funky cover-ups would be a big hit with the preteens who were likely to fit into them. The girls would split up her elegant suits, wearing the short skirts with sweaters and the jackets with jeans. She'd ended up with an embarrassing six boxes full, which Belinda would collect today.

She was stacking the last box on the sheltered porch when the roar of a sports car attracted her attention. It screeched to a halt in front of her gate. "Dexter!" she gasped as the tall, thin, elegantly dressed man emerged from the driver's seat. "What are you doing here?"

"I've come to get my dog," he said. His mouth was a compressed line above the sharp chin Sunny had come to dislike so intensely, along with the rest of his patrician appearance and demeanor. "You won't return my phone calls, so I drove up here to get him back. I'm in a hurry, Sunny. Don't give me any trouble." He advanced to the foot of the porch steps.

"Babe Ruth's my dog!"

The hard, thin line of lips curved in a humorless smile. "You never were very good with fine print, were you." He brandished a document in his hand. Sunny observed that he was dressed "for the country" in designer jeans, a white turtleneck, a lush brown leather bomber jacket and, of all things, brown hiking boots that said "new" all over them. Dexter worked out religiously at a gym, but she'd never seen him hike farther than the nearest taxi. "As my lawyer reminded you, the settlement agreement clearly states that the dog conveys with the apartment. *I'm* in the apartment now, and I want my dog." He stuck the papers back into his jacket pocket.

Sunny advanced on him, rage shooting up through her veins to heat her face and make her ears ring. "What happened to Marielle's allergy to dogs?"

His smile was slow, wide and humorless. "She's only allergic to them until they're housebroken."

"I see," Sunny hissed. "You didn't want a paper-trained, sock-chewing puppy that cried all night because you wouldn't let him sleep with you, but you *do* want a housebroken, beautifully behaved pedigreed dog to walk in the park so people can admire you for your good taste in pets. Forget your fine print, Dexter, because you can't have him! There's not a court in the world that would give him to you. That's not what having a dog is all about. It's about loving him and cuddling him and—"

"You're telling me you love the dog? All you did was gripe about having to take him. Don't lay this crap on me, Sunny."

"It's not crap, as you so elegantly put it," Sunny said

through clenched teeth. "I brought this dog up from his infancy, and you can't take him away now. Yes, I love him, too much to let him go. Get out of here before I call the cops. Cop."

Dexter gave her one last scornful look, snapped his fingers and said, "Hey, Babe, come to papa."

While Sunny screamed, "No!" Babe did what he did every time a guest came to her house. His eyes gleamed, his tail went up like a flag. His whole little body wagging a welcome, he bounded directly to Dexter and scrambled up into his arms.

THE NIGHT BEFORE, Colin had done something he never did: he drank too much, not *way* too much, just more than he'd drunk since graduate school, simply hoping for the first good night's sleep in a month. It worked, sort of. He overslept, and when he woke up he took four aspirin tablets, drank a pot of fully caffeinated coffee and decided his standoff with Sunny had to end.

He'd move with her to New York if that's what it took. Through her contacts with other interior designers, he would soon have all the work he could handle. He'd call his firm "Colin Blalock, Restorations." He'd put together a crew, train them to be master craftsmen and make piles of money. He'd love it once he got used to it, and while he got used to it, he'd be with Sunny.

He wouldn't see his parents as often, he'd miss out on whole stages of his nieces' and nephews' lives, but so be it. The inescapable fact was that nothing mattered anymore without Sunny. Why had it taken him so long to see it?

He'd go now, before the storm broke—or his courage to face the fiery little vixen failed him. Colin smiled ruefully. He would never again see sunshine or flames, red and gold autumn leaves or pine-strewn forest clearings without thinking about Sunny. With thoughts like that running through his head, he needed to keep her close enough to kiss. When the phone rang, he almost let it go, but what if it was Sunny? What if she'd read his mind and was calling to say—

"Colin!" It was his mother. Colin groaned. Time, which had been moving so slowly, seemed to be flying. "Are you there? Answer me this instant! You've got to get over here! It's an emergency! It looks as though Sunny's on her way back to New York! With her ex-husband! She's packed a lot of boxes. They're sitting on the porch, and he's here, ready to load…"

The telephone dangled from the hook, Margaret Blalock's voice still shrilling from the receiver.

"No," SUNNY SCREAMED again. "You can't take him!" She dashed toward Dexter, ready to claw his face with her fingernails. His arm shot out to hold her back. She reached for Babe, then realized how high off the ground he was in Dexter's grasp. He'd hurt himself if he fell. She boxed her way around Dexter to reach a better vantage point, but he effortlessly evaded her blows.

"I love that dog," Sunny cried, realizing all at once just how much she loved him, had always loved him. "He's still a baby. He needs me!"

"Look at him, Sunny," Dexter said coolly. "He's crazy about me, aren't you fella?" Babe wriggled in his arms, breathed hard in his face and gave him several wet kisses with his wide pink tongue. Dexter winced.

"He's like that with everybody," Sunny said. Now she was sobbing. "He's friendly, he's sweet, he loves people. He's never known anything but kindness, so he—" She couldn't finish the sentence. She made several more futile attempts to get her hands on Babe. "Give him to me, Dexter. He's going to fall. He'll break his leg. Put him down, Dexter, please!"

"I like him," said Dexter. "I'm taking him."

"The world is full of cairn terriers," Sunny sobbed. "You don't know Babe any better than you know them."

His smile was patronizing. "But as you pointed out earlier, they're not housebroken or trained yet. I guess I should say thanks for doing the dirty work." He took a few steps toward his car.

The sky grew darker, and a harsh wind blew from the west. Out of her head with anxiety, Sunny said, "It wasn't dirty work! It was fun, every minute of it, because—because he's mine!" She broke down completely just as a battered pickup truck screeched to a halt in front of Dexter's car, blocking the narrow street, and Colin slid smoothly out of it, slowly advancing toward her.

THERE WERE THE BOXES Sunny had packed, and there was the ex-husband Dexter carrying Babe Ruth to the car, but something was wrong with the scene. Confused, Colin tried to make sense out of the fact that Sunny was crying hysterically.

She'd probably broken a fingernail.

He stalked toward her. "Sunny, you can't leave until we've talked this over."

"Colin! Dexter came here to…"

"You don't want to go back to Dexter. So you sold the cottage. Are you so desperate for a place to live that you'd go back to a man you don't love? Think for a minute, Sunny. Think how dumb this is…"

He was startled when she stamped her foot. "What are you talking about?"

He gestured toward the boxes on the porch. "I'm talking about you leaving with Dexter," he growled. "I don't want you to leave with Dexter. I don't want you to leave with anybody! I don't want you to leave, period! That's what I'm talking about, damn it!"

"I'm not leaving with Dexter, dummy! He came to take Babe away!"

"You're not..."

"No!"

"He's trying to take Babe..."

"Yes!"

It sank in. She wasn't leaving. She was fighting for Babe, for something important, for someone she loved. "Sunny, I..."

"Don't stand there staring at me like a lovesick blue-eyed sheep!" Sunny yelled. "Do something!"

Colin pulled himself together. He'd do something, all right. Dexter had halted in his path to the car to view the scene with malevolent interest. Folding his arms across his chest, Colin took a step toward him. "You heard the lady. Put the dog down, and put him down easy."

"Don't sweet-talk him! Scare him!" Sunny snapped.

Colin forced himself to concentrate on the problem, not on the sob that took the snap out of her command.

"Tell this hick to move that...thing out of my way," said Dexter. His lips curled in a scornful assessment of the truck, and of Colin in his jeans, his faded green shirt and sheepskin jacket.

Colin took another step and Dexter's expression grew less scornful. "I said put the dog down. Don't make me say it a third time."

"Hey, fella," Dexter said, "I don't know who you are, but I don't need you telling me what to do. This dog is mine and there's not a damned thing you can do to keep me from taking him."

A bolt of lightning shot unexpectedly through the sky, closely followed by a deafening clap of thunder. In a swirl of brindle fur, a wild-eyed Babe flung himself out of Dexter's grasp and sailed through the air. Sunny screamed. Colin caught him in both hands and tried to hold on, but he wasn't the person Babe wanted in a crisis of this magnitude. Like a little whirlwind, he wrenched free and barreled into Sunny's legs, clawing at them. With one last sob she snatched him up.

"It's okay, baby, it's okay," she crooned, drying her face on his fur. "Mommy's got you. It's all right." She hid his face under her windbreaker and rocked him in her arms.

Colin saw her anew as she comforted the puppy. This is what his mother had sensed in Sunny: her sweetness, her warmth, her capacity for love, her need to be loved in return. Under his gaze she lifted still-frightened eyes to his. A flash of understanding passed between them before Dexter, his eyes and mouth hard as flint, advanced toward her.

"Don't take another step," Colin warned him. "Get in your car, put it in reverse, and back out of this town."

"Oh, bug off," Dexter muttered.

"Last chance," said Colin.

Dexter reached out for Babe.

"I'm sorry to have to do this," Colin said in the same calm tone, then drew back his fist and slammed Dexter in his sharp and elegant chin. Dexter sank slowly, a silly grin on his face, onto the fallen leaves.

The heavens opened and rain began to pelt down in big, heavy drops. Sunny leaned over Dexter's prone figure. "Is he dead?" she whispered.

"No," said Colin, "but he's having some interesting dreams." Effortlessly he slid his arms under Dexter's limp body, picked him up and balanced him on one arm while he opened the passenger door of the sports car.

"What's going on? You woke me up." The passenger seat shot forward and a breathtaking blonde, her face framed in a fur collar, stared at him.

"Marielle, I presume," said Colin. "We meet at last."

"Who are you? And what have you done to Dexter?

Dexter, baby!'' she cried. Her voice reminded him of maple syrup—straight from the refrigerator.

"You'll have to drive," Colin said politely. "Can you find reverse?"

Without a word, Marielle scurried around the car, never taking her eyes off Colin as he gently levered Dexter into a comfortable position. She hopped into the driver's seat and backed all the way down Main Street. In the near distance he heard the sound of hands clapping.

COLIN WHISKED SUNNY and Babe into the house. Just inside the door Sunny stopped to gaze up at him. Rain flattened his dark hair and streamed down his face, but his eyes were filled with the love she could now admit she wanted and needed above all else in the world.

"What timing," she murmured. "What made you come the very minute I needed you most?"

He smiled and enclosed Babe and her in one large, wet embrace. "ESP," he said. "Eternally Spying Parent. Sunny…" His words piled out on top of each other, as though he couldn't say them fast enough. "I should have paid attention to what you did, not what you said. You do care about the important things. Well, so do I. And you're the most important thing in my life. I can't expect you to change your entire agenda for me. I'll move to New York with you, if you'll have me."

Sunny jerked away to stare up at him, worried. She slicked a lock of wet hair out of her eyes and said, "No! My agenda has changed. I'm staying here."

"My agenda has changed, too, sweetheart. We're going to New York. You'll have your career, and it won't be long before I—"

"No!" Sunny stamped her foot again, spraying water on Colin's already soaked jeans. "We're staying here, where your business is, where you're happy, surrounded by our families and—"

"Sunny, I've thought this over very carefully. We're moving to New York and I won't take no for an answer."

"We're staying!"

"We're going!"

"Vermont!"

"New York!"

They glared at each other. Colin made his last stand. "If we go to the city we can live together for a while, get to know each other, let you have time to feel comfortable with the idea of getting married."

"I'm already comfortable with the idea. I want to get married immediately. I want those adorable Carters and their little Latham to have this cottage. They deserve it. I," she added firmly, "will move in with you."

"Why the rush?" His heart raced while he waited for the answer he knew she would give him.

"We have to get married," she said ominously, "before the ground freezes."

Colin folded his arms tightly around his shivering woman and her shivering dog. Exuberant laughter rose in his throat. "Sunny, you are going to make my life miserable," he said. When she wasn't making him sublimely happy. He lowered his mouth to hers and kissed her.

She drew back, picking hair off her lower lip. "Colin," she complained, "we've got to do something different with this dog."

Epilogue

SUNNY WAVED GOODBYE to Bev and little Josh, then gazed
after Elizabeth as she and Latham crossed the village green
to Woodbine Cottage. Returning to the garden behind the
larger, older house Colin had just finished restoring, she
slid into the space on the wooden swing between Margaret
and Starlight.

"Isn't this divine?" she said. "No plumbers, no electri-
cians, just us." Rosamond still held the garden hose Josh
and Latham had been playing in while Babe, matted and
quite naked, romped through the spray and Muffler glared
down at the scene from a low branch of the apple tree.

"This will be the first time you've lived without a restoration going on around you," Margaret said. "You deserve it."

"Your father is a bad influence on Colin," Starlight said
disapprovingly. "The two of them think there is no house
in the world they can't make livable again."

"There isn't," said Sunny, smiling at her own memories.
"I cried when Colin showed me the farmhouse, but I ended
up being so happy there that I cried when he told me we
were moving here."

"Three houses in four years," said Margaret. "Surely
this is it for a while."

"Darned right it is," said Sunny. "My design business
is thriving and I want to enjoy the calm and relaxation of
spending other people's money." What she wanted was a
baby, but it seemed only polite to mention it to Colin first.

It was time to share the happiness they'd found with each other. It was time for Babe to have a baby brother or sister before he got too accustomed to being the only child. "Where are Colin and Poppa anyway?" she complained.

As though in answer to her summons, Colin arrived with her father in his increasingly careworn pickup, striding over, tall, tanned and energetic, to drop a kiss on her sunwarmed head that sent a shiver straight down her spine.

Rosamond turned off the hose, Colin and Laurence turned to look at the women, and a pregnant silence fell over the yard. Instinctively Sunny got up, seeking a better fighting position. She cleared her throat. "What kept you two?"

Colin attempted a blasé gesture. "Ah. We, well, we had a few minutes, so…"

"The original Latham house is for sale," Laurence said impatiently. "The big brick place in Latham Center…"

"No," said Sunny.

"My goodness, would you look at the time," said Margaret. "We must be getting home. All of us," she added pointedly.

"…that I've always wanted to get back into family hands," said Colin. "We dropped in to look it over, and it's…"

"You'll be along in a minute, Laurence?" Starlight said threateningly.

"Under no circumstances," said Sunny.

"…fantastic!" said Laurence. "Built in seventeen-ninety! And the original…"

"I don't want to hear another word," said Sunny.

"Laurence! Come! You, too, Babe!"

"…ceilings, and chimney, and fireplaces, and maple parquet floors—they're all there underneath the acoustical tile and plywood and Sheetrock and carpeting…"

"Parquet floors?" said Sunny.

They were at last alone in the garden. "All it needs is a little TLC," said Colin. "It sits on two acres of land, surrounded by woods..." He paused, gazing at Sunny significantly.

"Can you see Mrs. Forrester's chicken coop when the maples lose their leaves?" asked Sunny. Her voice had softened.

Their eyes locked in acknowledgement of the passion that only grew with time. "Yes," Colin said softly, and moved close to put his arms around her.

"If we do this absurd, ridiculous, self-indulgent thing," said Sunny, "I insist that our baby be born there."

He drew back. "Sunny! Darling! Is it true? Are you..."

"Not yet," she said. Her eyebrows arched suggestively. "But if you will at last give in and tell me what happened to North Latham, maybe by morning..."

"You still don't understand Vermont," Colin sighed. "I've known you for less than five years. Maybe in another twenty or so..."

"Col-in!"

"Okay, then, after we've had a baby together," he said, and kissed her.

MEN at WORK

All work and no play?
Not these men!

January 1999
SOMETHING WORTH KEEPING by Kathleen Eagle
He worked with iron and steel, and was as wild as the mustangs that were his passion. She was a high-class horse trainer from the East. Was her gentle touch enough to tame his unruly heart?

February 1999
HANDSOME DEVIL by Joan Hohl
His roguish good looks and intelligence drew women like magnets, but Luke Branson was having too much fun to marry again. Then Selena McInnes strolled before him and turned his life upside down!

March 1999
STARK LIGHTNING by Elaine Barbieri
The boss's daughter was ornery, stubborn and off-limits for cowboy Branch Walker! But Valentine was also nearly impossible to resist. Could they negotiate a truce...or a surrender?

Available at your favorite retail outlet!

MEN AT WORK™

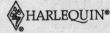 

Sexy, desirable and...a daddy?

THE  AUSTRALIANS

Stories of romance Australian-style, guaranteed to fulfill that sense of adventure!

This February 1999 look for

Baby Down Under

by **Ann Charlton**

Riley Templeton was a hotshot Queensland lawyer with a reputation for ruthlessness and a weakness for curvaceous blondes. Alexandra Page was everything that Riley *wasn't* looking for in a woman, but when she finds a baby on her doorstep that leads her to the dashing lawyer, he begins to see the virtues of brunettes—and babies!

The Wonder from Down Under: where spirited women win the hearts of Australia's most independent men!

Available February 1999
at your favorite retail outlet.

HARLEQUIN®

Makes any time special ™

LOVE & LAUGHTER™

What's your favorite Valentine's Day present?

- ☐ A dozen red roses?
- ☐ Chocolates, chocolates and more chocolates?
- ☐ A delectable, heartwarming romantic comedy that is also 100% fat free?

If you chose the romantic comedy, then have we got a treat for you for Valentine's Day!

Coming in February 1999:

#61 COURTING CUPID by Charlotte Maclay

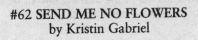

#62 SEND ME NO FLOWERS
by Kristin Gabriel

*Happy Valentine's Day
from Love & Laughter!*

Available wherever Harlequin books are sold.

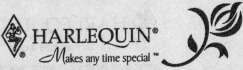